A VEXING
WOMAN

Amelia Smarts

Published by Amelia Smarts
ameliasmarts.com

Smarts, Amelia
A Vexing Woman
ISBN: 9798388496669

Cover Design by Designrans
Image by The Killion Group

This book is intended for adults only. Spanking
and other sexual activities represented in this
book are fantasies only, intended for adults.

CHAPTER ONE

Texas, 1897

As the sun rose to greet another day, Maxwell Harrison hammered a hot strip of iron over his anvil, shaping it into a U. "Add some coal to the forge, Jim," he said to the lad who sat on a bench in the blacksmith's shop, organizing tools into the new wooden toolkit Max had built. Like a doctor who traveled around town with medicine to fix people, Max traveled with tools to fix just about everything else.

Jim set his small task aside to do as Max instructed. They were expecting two newly broke horses for shoeing that day, so they needed to shape eight horseshoes. After ensuring the mustangs were properly shod, they needed to fix an axle on a rancher's buggy.

Max had been a blacksmith or blacksmith-in-training for most of his thirty-four years. Nearly as soon as he could pick up a hammer, his father began teaching him the trade. Because much of the work Max and his father used to do, like sculpting nails, could now be done by machines in the factories found in bigger cities, Max's work evolved into more than just blacksmithing. The folks of Porter, Texas, could count on him to fix or build just about anything made of wood, metal, or leather.

Max taught everything he knew to Jim, his sixteen-year-old apprentice and unofficial charge. The son of a man who liked to swing his fists as much as he liked to sling back whiskey, Jim had been living with Max for nearly two years at Max's insistence. Jim's father had agreed to the arrangement, provided that Max pay him for the use of his son. It was ridiculous, Max knew, to teach the boy the tools of the trade, and on top of that pay for his service and room and board, but he couldn't stomach another day of Jim showing up with a black eye, so he'd agreed to the terms without much argument.

Max heard the hinges of the heavy door to the shop whine behind him. Expecting Jack with his two horses, he was surprised when he turned to find Marshal Jake Huntley striding in.

Max set the hammer and half-bent horseshoe on the anvil and removed his work glove from his right hand. "Howdy, marshal. What brings you here?"

The marshal shook his outstretched hand and spoke hurriedly. "I must ask a favor of you,

Max, and before you answer, let me say two things. One, I wouldn't ask unless I urgently needed it, and two, it might not be entirely unpleasant. It involves the company of a rather fetching young woman, if her picture is any clue." He handed Max a photograph the size of a playing card.

Max studied it. The woman in the photograph who frowned back at him was certainly pretty, though she had a stiff look about her with a back held very straight. Her chin tilted upward just a bit too high to appear biddable, or even friendly.

"What sort of favor, marshal?"

"That's to be Porter's new schoolmarm. She's on her way from Boston, and I'm supposed to meet her at the train station in Arcadia tomorrow morning. Trouble is, I can't make it. Not ten minutes ago I received a wire from the sheriff in Dallas that two baddies are headed here with a law posse in pursuit. The sheriff requested that I form a posse of my own to cut them off at the pass."

"So you want me to fetch a girl, not join your posse? I'll try not to let that injure my manly pride, marshal."

The marshal let out an amused snort. "I've never even seen you pack iron, Max, so I wouldn't ask you to join in a hunt for outlaws. If you leave now, you'll reach Arcadia by nightfall. Take a room there overnight and meet the schoolmarm in the morning. The county will pay for your boarding, of course."

Max scratched his head. "I can shoot a gun, you know. I'm not a terrible aim either. But, well, I suppose I could have Jim attend to the work today and head for Arcadia. I just need—"

"Great," the marshal interrupted, turning to leave. "Appreciate it, Max." He walked at a quick clip toward the door.

"Hey, marshal," Max called. "Mind telling me her name?"

"It's Charlotte. Charlotte Rose. Give her my regrets for being unable to meet her," he said, and left as abruptly out the door as he came in it.

Max instructed Jim on what to do while he was away and went about fitting his buggy with food, water, and a few emergency supplies, including his old Remington, his new toolkit, and a quilt. In less than an hour, he climbed into the buggy seat and directed his horse toward the path headed east.

He studied the picture of Charlotte Rose. She was truly beautiful. She had almond-shaped eyes and long hair that fell to her waist. The photograph captured her in a seated position from head to toe. Max's eyes lingered on her breasts, the ample size of which couldn't be concealed despite being draped with modest clothing.

"Settle down there, Max," he muttered to himself.

He stared at the haughty lift of her chin, trying to convince himself it didn't give him a bit of a thrill. She looked like a handful in more than one way. His thoughts wandered to his ex-wife, who ten years ago had traveled from the east to the west, intent on starting a new life, but realized after a year of marriage to Max that she didn't belong in the crude landscape. She left him and returned to the big city she came from, and he didn't try to stop her.

Max wondered about the woman in the photograph. Would she be cowed by the hard work, lack of certain leisure activities, and rugged culture? Something in her eyes told him she just might make it.

* * *

Charlotte stood with some difficulty when the train screeched to a halt. Her legs were cramped and she felt hot and in need of rest, despite having hardly moved in days of travel. She'd had little opportunity to stretch her legs other than when she paced the confines of the train car. Looking out the window at the smattering of people on the platform, she tried to locate a man with a badge. She didn't see anyone who looked like a marshal, which was the occupation of the man she'd been informed would meet her, but that didn't mean anything. She knew that lawmen in the west didn't wear uniforms, unlike in Boston where jobs and manners were far more structured. Charlotte was struck by the overall simple nature of everything from the signs to the bushes lacking flowers. The place was crude, severe, and without ornament.

Like many times previously in the last few days, she again felt a knot in her stomach over the decision to throw herself into a place so unknown to her. She already missed her mother terribly. Her mother had sent Charlotte off with her full blessing, blubbering through her tears about how proud she was of her only child. Her father hadn't said goodbye, but that wasn't surprising. He'd never cared about her. One of her motivations for leaving was to escape him and men like him.

As she stepped down onto the platform, carrying a sturdy black carpetbag that held all of her earthly possessions, she looked around. Jealousy gripped her as she watched one of the women she'd traveled with run into the open arms of a beaming man. Charlotte felt very alone and insignificant in comparison.

She noticed a man striding in her direction. He wore a black Stetson that cast a shadow over his face, a blue bandanna around his neck, faded denim trousers, and a white shirt that buttoned down the front. She wrinkled her nose as he neared. White was clearly not the right color to wear in this dusty town, since his shirt appeared more tan than white in some places. She briefly looked down at her dress. It was her finest. Its taffeta skirt was pink, and the bodice was made of black crushed velvet with white lace trim that also didn't appear as white as it should. The silk of the skirt and the three petticoats under it felt terribly heavy and uncomfortable in the heat of Texas's summer, and she wished for a brief moment to be wearing one of the light cotton frocks donned by the women around her, as unattractive as they were.

The man took off his hat as he neared. "Miss Charlotte Rose?" he asked in a deep, lazy drawl, so very different from her own accent.

Charlotte felt a moment's surprise when she saw his unshaded face. The man was very handsome in a rugged, unassuming way, with dark brows and thick dark hair. Stubble dotted his pronounced jawline. His full lips turned up in a half smile, and he regarded her with twinkling green eyes. She suddenly felt glad to be wearing her best dress.

"Yes, I'm Miss Rose. And you are?"

"Maxwell Harrison. Call me Max."

Charlotte felt disappointed upon learning he was not the marshal in charge of fetching her, and she bristled at his greeting. "That wouldn't be proper, Mr. Harrison, as we only just met. And at the risk of sounding impolite, I must say I don't know why we're meeting. I'm here to meet Marshal Jake Huntley."

His eyes seemed to twinkle more after her reproach. "The marshal sends his regrets. He had an emergency and asked me to fetch you, so I'll be escorting you to Porter. My buggy is just this way.

I'll carry your bag."

He reached out to take it, but Charlotte clutched the handle tighter and moved the bag slightly away from him. She frowned. "I beg your pardon, Mr. Harrison, but I wasn't informed of this change in plans. How am I to know you tell the truth? I don't know you from Adam. You could be a thief or ruffian, and you expect me to allow you to escort me on a journey to the boondocks?"

She could see that he struggled not to smile at her rebuff, which irritated her. She didn't see any humor in her valid concerns. He cleared his throat. "Porter isn't Boston, Charlotte, but it's not the boondocks either, which is why we have the need for a lady such as yourself. There are plenty of people there, including plenty of children who need a schoolmarm. Do I look like a ruffian or thief?"

"Please be so kind as to call me Miss Rose." She paused, wondering if she should hold her tongue, but the man had irritated her and so she continued. "Are you sure you want me to answer that question regarding your appearance, Mr. Harrison?"

He smiled then, which crinkled the corners of his eyes. He removed something from his shirt pocket and handed it to her. "The marshal gave me your photograph so I'd know what you look like. Not that I needed it. Your appearance hollers greenhorn from a mile away. Is your photo proof enough he sent me?"

Charlotte glanced at it, then tucked it under her dress near her bosom. She glared at the man, who, to his credit, did not remove his gaze from her face, despite her hand resting near one of her finest assets. "If my appearance hollers greenhorn, then your appearance screams ruffian, Mr. Harrison."

He laughed. "I might just be a ruffian. I don't have a woman at home nagging me about my appearance and manners."

Everything she said seemed to amuse him, which perplexed Charlotte. She was known for her beauty, not for her humor. She sighed, feeling much more fatigued than worried about his character by this point. He seemed to notice her weariness. The amusement left his face, replaced by resolve. He put his hat back on his head and took the bag from her hand. She didn't try to stop him.

"Enough blather. Come along now. You still have a spell of travel before you can rest properly." He walked toward what Charlotte assumed was his buggy, which looked very small and dirty. She followed him. When they reached it, he placed her bag in the back and picked up an old army canteen, which he handed to her. "Drink some water," he ordered. "Are you hungry?"

Charlotte took a long drink. Her thirst properly quenched, she said, "That depends on what you have. Somehow I doubt you have anything I'd find edible." She knew she was being rude, but his casual manner and presumptuous nature rankled her. She was accustomed to being spoken to in courtly tones, not laughed at and ordered about.

Max raised an eyebrow slowly and studied her for a moment. "I've got bread, jerky, and apples, if that suits your fancy, but we can stop at a restaurant before leaving if it doesn't. Which would you prefer, Charlie?"

Charlotte could hardly believe her ears. How dare he not only use her first name, but also a bastardized, male version of it? She lifted her chin and gave him a withering look. "I informed you that I prefer to be called Miss Rose, not Charlotte, and *certainly* not Charlie."

"Yes I know you did, Charlie, and that was your first mistake. Your second is not answering my question about whether you're hungry. That could try a lesser man's patience."

Charlotte scowled. "I fail to see how asking to be regarded properly is a mistake, Mr. Harrison."

Max folded his arms in front of him and leaned against the back of the buggy. "I'll tell you how. You shouldn't let people know what raises your bristles if you wish to keep that smart mouth of yours. Folks out here won't appreciate you looking down your nose at them. You do that to a man, he'll find a way to annoy you, as I managed to do without even hardly trying."

Charlotte's mouth hung open for a moment before she closed it and set her jaw angrily.

The man had actually lectured her about proper behavior, despite his own being anything but! His impertinence overshadowed his good looks, and she decided that she didn't think much of the brazen man she was unfortunate enough to be dependent on for the next eight hours.

"I'll do without your chicken feed and forego the restaurant. The sooner I can be alone in my new dwelling, the better." She lifted her skirts and stormed to the front of the buggy. She stopped and stared up at the seat. "Where are the steps, Mr. Harrison? How am I to get up?" she asked, genuinely flummoxed. "Am I to run and jump, or would you have me clamor up the muddy wheel?"

She heard a coughed laugh before she felt her feet leave the ground. Max deposited her on the seat like one might a sack of flour, then rounded the buggy and climbed up next to her. Without a word, he released the brake, clucked to the horse, and slapped the reins on her back. The horse moved forward at a quick clip.

Charlotte's heart beat wildly. She felt outraged, but she also felt something else— a fluttering in her stomach. No man had ever dared touch her without her consent. Men were generally shy around her. She knew she was a beauty and that her beauty rendered men weak, yet here was a man who, after minutes of knowing her, had not only scolded her but also taken her into his arms. If he thought she was beautiful and felt shy over it, he certainly didn't let on.

"I suppose it's considered proper out here for a man to grab a lady's person without her consent. Is that the case, Mr. Harrison, or are you unique in that respect?"

He chuckled. "Proper isn't a big concern of most men out here, I'd say."

"Oh? And what concerns a man such as yourself?"

He raked her with his gaze from head to toe before answering. "My concern at the moment is getting a young lady home to rest before she keels over. You look flushed and clear tuckered out. Perhaps even a mite feverish."

"I feel fine, thank you." As she said it, she knew it was a lie. She felt warmer than she'd ever felt and the thought of enduring eight hours of travel in the oppressive heat filled her with something like despair.

"Do you have something to wear other than those fancy duds?"

Charlotte felt her cheeks grow even hotter hearing his words. "What's wrong with what I'm wearing?"

He sighed. "You have a problem answering questions, don't you, Charlie? I'm only asking because you might feel more comfortable in lighter clothing. How many petticoats are you wearing under that gown?"

Charlotte gasped. "Mr. Harrison, there's a reason a woman's unmentionables are called just that. I'll thank you to remember your manners, if you ever had them."

He let out a noise that sounded much like a growl. "Do you have something to wear other than that heavy silk dress? Just answer me that." He frowned at her, then added with sarcasm, "If you please, good lady."

Charlotte gaped at him a moment before lifting her chin higher and responding, "I do have another dress in my bag, but I assure you I am fine in this."

He shook his head but relented with another sigh. "If you say so."

They rode in silence for some time. After what seemed like hours of travel, Charlotte felt dizzy and nauseated. She inwardly cursed her stubborn pride and wished she'd changed into her lighter calico dress when the man suggested it. She loathed the thought of admitting he was right, so she didn't speak of her distress, even when her breathing became panting and sweat dripped from her face onto her hands. She felt her muscles weaken. She soon had no strength to remain upright and balance herself in the seat, which jerked at every bump in the road. She slumped toward the edge of the buggy and then felt Max's hand grasp her wrist and yank her back.

She passed out after that because the next thing she knew, she was lying on a quilt next to the wagon with Max on his knees by her side. "I was a fool to listen to you," he snarled. "Damn and blast!" His voice seemed far away. "I need to take off your dress. I'm sorry, but you have a touch of heatstroke and you're burning up."

She offered no resistance as he stripped her to her shift and removed all but one petticoat, which he mercifully left on her body. He removed her shoes and stockings, and she felt relief when the air touched her toes. He poured water from the canteen over her face, neck, and along her arms. He did the same to her feet and legs up to her knees. As her body felt relief from the anguish, her mind became anguished over the humiliating situation.

He soaked his bandanna and tied it loosely around her neck, then slid an arm under her shoulders and lifted her to a seated position. He held the canteen to her lips, and she drank a few sips. "Drink some more," he ordered, and Charlotte obeyed.

"Feel better?" he asked, his eyes boring into hers.

She nodded and averted her eyes from his penetrating stare. With her arms, she covered her chest, which was as good as naked. The water he'd poured on her had rendered her thin white shift transparent. She hung her head. Max stood, retrieved her bag, and located her lighter dress. Handing it to her, he said, "Put this on, then take off your petticoat from under it. We'll be on our way after that." He dropped her bag and walked to the other side of the buggy to give her privacy, which would have been laughable after he'd seen her stripped to her underclothes, if it wasn't so humiliating.

Charlotte felt knocked down more than a few pegs, but she still didn't like being told what to do, especially about her own clothing. The least he could have done was explain to her politely what he thought was best instead of ordering her around. He might also have asked before rummaging through her personal belongings to locate her other dress, and he might have placed her bag on the quilt instead of dropping it in the dirt. Insufferable man! Her ire toward him returned as she stood and slipped the dress over her shoulders.

Upon buttoning the last of the buttons up to her chest, she addressed him in hesitant tone, knowing her words would displease him and unsure about the wisdom of doing so. "I will leave my petticoat on, Mr. Harrison. This dress is improper otherwise."

For an awful moment, there was no sound or movement. Then she saw his shadow appear near the back of the buggy and shortly after Max himself approaching her, wearing a fierce scowl. He stopped a horse length away.

"Vexing woman! If you possess a lick of sense, you will remove your petticoat. Then you will obey any other order I give you from now until I get you home. Give me any more trouble before then, and I'll turn you over my knee. And so help me, there won't be a petticoat, or a dress, or anything else between my hand and your high-and-mighty backside when I spank some common sense into you."

Charlotte felt horrified. She gulped, then exclaimed, "You wouldn't dare, Mr. Harrison!" Tears suddenly stung her eyes.

"Oh, but I would, Charlie." He moved a step toward her. "Maybe I ought to smack your bottom a few times right now to prove it."

She took a step back and held out a hand to stop his approach. "That won't be necessary, Mr. Harrison. I will do your bidding. I see I have no choice, since you're devoid of the manners that befit a gentleman and would feel no compunction over beating me."

She sniffled as she bent to remove her petticoat from under her dress. This place was like a foreign country, so very different from Boston, and she suddenly felt like she'd never be able to adapt, if all the men around were like the one standing in front of her scowling. After folding her petticoat in half a couple of times, she held it against her chest and gazed at him sorrowfully. She felt her lower lip tremble and told herself not to humiliate herself further by allowing the sobs to overtake her.

Max's expression softened as he sighed and closed the gap between them. Lifting her into his arms yet again, he said, "I wouldn't beat you, honey. A spanking is not a beating. Thank you for obeying me, though, so as not to learn the difference today." He placed her on the buggy seat gently, then removed the petticoat from her limp hands and stuffed it into her bag.

CHAPTER TWO

Max felt his heartbeat slow to a normal pace soon after resuming their journey. Dealing with a feverish, unconscious woman in the middle of nowhere had given him a fright, and he felt angry with himself for allowing her to get to that point. Unlike him, she hadn't a clue about how to care for herself in a place where temperatures rose to over a hundred degrees in the summer. He should have insisted much earlier that she change into appropriate clothing.

His fear now gone, he worried about how to contend with the distraught and humiliated woman sitting next to him. He didn't like seeing the little spitfire he'd met on the platform in such a state. He'd felt much more comfortable when she was giving him lip and showing a bit of pluck. Now she was subdued and depressed. She hung her head and stared at her hands in her lap, sniffling quietly every so often.

He wondered what her story was. She was

beyond beautiful; she was utterly breathtaking. She could have batted her eyelashes at just about any man and found herself in a comfortable position for life. Instead, she'd traveled alone to a hard place, intent on earning a living for herself. Max thought about asking her what made her want to leave home, but he didn't think he could bear it if his question caused her to cry and feel regret.

He reached into his pack and selected the finest looking apple. "Eat this," he said, handing it to her.

Without a word, she slowly took the piece of fruit. She studied it for a moment, rubbed it down thoroughly with the skirt of her dress, and took a bite. He felt glad that she was getting some nourishment, but he'd hoped for a bit of an argument, like she'd offered him about everything else prior to that point. He recognized that she was heeding his order to obey or else endure a spanking. He should have felt glad about that, but he felt strangely bereft. He worried that he might have broken her spirit somehow.

"Can I do anything to make you more comfortable, Charlie?"

"No, Mr. Harrison," she said in a voice that sounded dangerously close to tears.

"I wish you'd call me Max."

"Why?"

"I don't know, exactly. It just seems odd to be called Mr. Harrison."

She didn't respond immediately, but when she eventually did, her accusatory tone provided him with relief. "I suspect it's so you feel better about using and abusing my Christian name."

"I reckon that has something to do with it."

"Well, you'll get no such satisfaction from me, Mr. Harrison. I think we're familiar enough as it is, much to my humiliation, without being on a first-name basis."

He winced and rubbed the back of his neck. "I wish I could say something to make you feel better about what happened. Honestly, there's no reason for you to feel humiliated, honey. You're new here. It's my fault I didn't insist that you change into better clothes before you became ill. Your stubborn pride didn't help, of course, but I should have ignored it."

She swallowed a bite of apple. "I suppose that's your attempt at an apology."

"Something like that."

Her resignation disappeared, replaced by all the outrage he'd witnessed from her previously. "I don't forgive you, Mr. Harrison. Further, I'll thank you not to call me honey or Charlie or any other name for me that forms inside your impertinent, hard head."

Max couldn't suppress a chuckle. "Sorry, honey, but you'll get no such satisfaction from me either. Charlie suits you. It suits you just fine."

She huffed and tossed the half-eaten apple into the weeds by the side of the path. "That was horrid. I've had lemons that were sweeter," she reported.

He smirked but managed not to laugh outright. Out of the corner of his eye, he saw her chin lift, and he felt much better about the situation. He ceased speaking to her, allowing her to be left alone with her thoughts. He knew she'd feel better once he got her home and out of his presence.

He thought it would be best if he didn't try to see her again. That saddened him, as he would have liked to get to know her better, but he felt it much more important that she regain her dignity. He wanted her to thrive in Porter, where she'd no doubt struggle enough. She didn't need him in her life as a reminder of her first sour taste of the west.

* * *

The morning after he escorted Charlotte to her room at the boardinghouse, Max returned to the monotony of his daily life. Missing two days of work set him back, even though Jim had been able to shoe the two horses and repair the wagon axle himself. Upon returning to his shop, Max faced three new jobs. The seamstress needed new hangers, the marshal asked for a length of chain, and the saloon owner wanted a new poker table.

A week after he bid Charlotte goodbye and good luck, Max still couldn't get her off his mind.

He remembered the look and feel of her soft skin as he cooled her down with water and the way the light of the sun highlighted the chestnut hair she had pinned in an elaborate bun on her head. He reckoned a lovelier creature didn't exist anywhere on earth. Her personality charmed him too. Her sharp tongue amused him, but it didn't fool him. He could tell that she used it to veil her vulnerability, and he admired her grit and ability to stand up for herself. That would serve her well in Porter.

He wanted more than just about anything to see her again, but he believed she wouldn't want to see him. He'd witnessed her in a compromised state, which he knew to someone as proud as her, likely stung terribly. He felt an ache in his chest when he remembered the way her eyes filled with tears when he threatened to spank her. Perhaps he'd been a bit too strict in that scolding he gave her. He still thought her stubborn pride warranted a good spanking, but she seemed to need a good hug too, and he wished to give her both.

Jim interrupted his thoughts. "Max, might I leave early today? I have something that needs doing before nightfall."

Max straightened from where he was bent adding coal to the furnace and regarded the boy. "Is it something important, Jim? We're awfully busy."

"Yes, sir. It is."

"Care to tell me what?"

Jim looked down and shifted his weight to one foot. When he didn't respond, Max frowned. It was unlike Jim to keep secrets from him, and it was also unlike him to ask for favors. He was eager to please, often to a fault. For the first few months of his apprenticeship, the boy was so afraid of doing something wrong that he frequently made errors because of it. It took him a long time to stop cowering after a mistake.

Jim had eventually realized that Max wouldn't treat him harshly like his father did. Ironically, as soon as he stopped worrying about making mistakes, he all but stopped making them. He'd become a talented blacksmith and showed promise in carpentry. Jim still made every effort to please Max, but did so by that time out of love and loyalty as opposed to fear.

Max held a strip of iron in the fire of the forge. "You'd let me know if you were in some kind of trouble, wouldn't you, Jim?"

He hesitated for a moment, then responded, "Yes."

"All right then, leave early if you must."

Jim thanked him and they discussed the work that needed to be done. Next on their list was the saloon's poker table. Max left the shop and headed toward the bar, slowing his stride as he passed the schoolhouse in the hopes of catching a glimpse of Charlotte, but she didn't venture outside if she was there at all. School wasn't in session for another couple of weeks.

Arriving at his destination, Max swung open one of the double doors, walked in, and planted himself on a stool at the bar. Piano music and laughter filled his ears as he exchanged pleasantries with the bartender and ordered a cold beer.

Jesse, the owner of the saloon, spotted Max and wandered over to him. "I hope you're here about the poker table," he said with a smile. "My customers have been complaining about it for months now. It sure could use an upgrade."

"Let's have a look," Max responded, and downed the rest of his beer. They walked to the round table covered with tattered green felt. Three men sat around it.

"Boys, you'll have to pause your game for a minute. Max needs to have a look at the table."

The men stood and moved back. Max ran his hand across the top, then crouched and shook each of the red cedar legs. He stood. "You don't need a new table, Jesse. This wood is solid. It's just got some loose bolts, and the felt is bad. I'll get the right cut of material from the seamstress and nail it in properly. I'll also replace and tighten the bolts so the table doesn't wobble anymore. That's all that needs doing."

Jesse thanked him, and Max joined the men in a quick game on the unsteady table. Two of the men, Sam and Tom, were ranch hands, and the other was a man with a reputation for being the town drunk, an affable older fellow by the name of

Pete. Max dealt. As he fanned his cards in front of him, Sam spoke out loud the very subject on Max's mind.

"You fellers catch a glimpse of the new schoolmarm? She sure is a looker."

Max felt his muscles tense, and he suddenly couldn't read the cards he was staring at.

Pete nodded. "She stays at the same boardinghouse as me, so I see her in passing. Nice gal."

"Don't much care about whether she's nice," Sam said, laughing. "Her nice rack is what I noticed." The other two men joined him in laughter.

Max seethed at the casual mention of Charlotte's body. He felt protective, which surprised him, and also possessive, which surprised him more. Neither were appropriate feelings, since she was far from being his to protect or possess.

Tom chortled and added his two cents. "It's those highfalutin shakesters that are downright dirty when it comes to a roll in the hay. That's been my experience, anyway."

"Right," Pete said, rolling his eyes. "I'm sure you have lots of experience bedding classy broads."

"Raise," Max said through gritted teeth, throwing another chip in the pile.

"What about you, Max?" Sam said. "You've been quiet on the subject of the schoolmarm."

Max shrugged and feigned interest in his

cards. "I fetched her from the train station in Arcadia when she arrived and brought her here. I like her well enough."

Sam whistled. "All that time in the company of a right smart piece of calico, and all you've got to say is you like her well enough? The smoke from the forge must be addling your brain and softening your cock, blacksmith."

Tom laughed loudly and slapped his palm on the table a few times.

Pete drew a card. "Maybe he's sweet on her, and that's why he don't wanna talk about her," he remarked wisely.

Max set his cards face up on the table. He couldn't concentrate on the game and accepted defeat. "I'd prefer if my cock and the schoolmarm's assets stayed clear out of your filthy mind, Sam. Good day, gentlemen." He rose to his feet and walked away. "I use that term loosely," he flung over his shoulder before he flung the saloon door open and strode outside. He heard the sound of the men's laughter fade as the distance between him and the saloon grew.

Thanks to Sam, the image of Charlotte's breasts under her wet shift entered his thoughts, suddenly making it very uncomfortable for him to walk. When she'd been suffering from heatstroke, he'd been too afraid she wouldn't recover to spend any time studying her chest, but now he couldn't help but think about the two glorious mounds, so ample and yet rebelliously perky, a fitting match to her rebellious personality. He groaned and tried to subdue his unwelcome lust. He needed to get the schoolmarm off his mind, and he wasn't doing a very good job of it. When he wasn't lusting after her body, he found himself worrying about how she was getting on in the new town on her own. He hoped she was doing better than his ex-wife had done.

Against his better judgment, he walked in the direction of the boardinghouse, hoping again to catch a glimpse of her. He didn't intend to call on her, but he wanted to at least see her in passing. He thought if he could just do that, he might be put at ease and able to remove her from his thoughts. The way she carried herself would provide a clue as to how she was faring in Porter, and that was his main concern.

As he neared the house, he slowed, and his blood ran cold. Coming out the front door was Simon Evans, Jim's abusive father. Before that moment, Max hadn't been aware that he was boarding there, and he felt a surge of alarm upon realizing Simon lived in such close proximity to Charlotte. The man was charming and, being from Baltimore, had the eastern manners she was accustomed to. Max knew that Simon's manners only served to hide his cruelty, but Charlotte wouldn't know that, nor would she know that Simon's wife fled his fists a couple of years ago and that women at the saloon refused to entertain him after more than one report of a vicious sexual encounter.

Simon and Max walked toward each other and stopped to exchange obligatory words of greeting and small talk. "Hello, Max," he said. "How's my son doing at blacksmithing?" He spoke the name of the trade with a sneer as though it were a vulgar word.

"Very well. He's a smart lad," Max responded, forcing a polite tone to carry his words. One of Max's biggest fears was being unable to protect Jim if Simon decided to exercise his parental rights and insist on the boy's return. Max knew that if he could remain cordial with the lad's father, their arrangement was in less danger of changing.

"I will call on you to get my pay at the end of the month," Simon said with a false smile. "I'm no longer living outside of town, as you can see."

Max gave him a nod. "I didn't know you moved to the boardinghouse. I hear it's a nice place."

"It has its selling points," he said with a smirk.

Max didn't care to hear what those points were, fearing he already knew they included the presence of a beautiful new resident. "Take care, Simon," he said, and continued on his way.

He walked past the residence of Simon and Charlotte, his hands closing into fists as he did. With much difficulty, he squashed his instinct to hunt Charlotte down and warn her about her neighbor. Doubling back after a sufficient amount of time to avoid having to run into Simon again, he headed toward his shop, trying to settle his consternation. It bothered him knowing that Charlotte was just Simon's type—young, book-learned, and beautiful.

Aw, hell, he thought, kicking a pebble on the ground. Who was he kidding? She was every man's type, and he couldn't very well go around beating them all off with a stick. He found some comfort in telling himself that Simon wouldn't hurt Charlotte unless they became more than acquaintances, which wouldn't happen immediately. It would only be after charming her into his clutches that Simon would show his true colors. The thought of it sent a shiver down his spine. Max decided that he would keep his eyes and ears open. He would talk to people in town and keep abreast of the situation. If he learned that Charlotte and Simon were becoming familiar, he would step in and warn Charlotte of Simon's character, despite it not being his business to do so.

CHAPTER THREE

The morning following her rough journey with Max, Charlotte awoke feeling better than she had for days. Before collapsing into a deep, twelve-hour sleep, she'd eaten a hearty meal of fried chicken, sweet rolls, and corn. Max had escorted her to her room at the boardinghouse, bid her farewell, and then showed up an hour later. He knocked and announced himself while she was crying on her new bed, feeling hungry, alone, and regretful over her choice to move west. When she realized he'd returned and was standing outside her door, she quickly dried her eyes and donned a robe over her nightdress. She opened the door to find him holding a platter of supper for her to eat in her room. It was a kind gesture. She felt a flood of gratefulness and a desire to throw herself into his arms. Instead, she thanked him politely and waited until he left to dissolve into tears again.

Despite how much the man needled her, it

became clear to Charlotte upon reflection in the morning that there was unmistakable kindness and respect in his every action. He'd taken care of her when she was ill, done his best not to embarrass her unnecessarily, and then had seen to it that she was well fed on her first night in town. He was the only person not a stranger in the strange new place, and she hoped he would call on her. Days passed, however, and he didn't visit. She tried not to let it bother her, but she felt rejected. Her time with him had been far from her finest hour, but she thought he might be at least mildly interested in her well-being. She even flattered herself into thinking that he might fancy her. With every day that passed, however, it became more obvious to her that he didn't.

She got to know other people in town. She met the marshal, who was nearly as handsome as Max, and the marshal's wife, Missy, who baked a cherry pie for her as a welcoming gift. Her fellow boarders were friendly too. She spoke occasionally with a boarder named Simon Evans, who was from Maryland. One morning, a week after her arrival, he asked her to breakfast in the dining room of the house, and she accepted.

At first she felt grateful for his company. She thought it might help alleviate some of her homesickness, but she soon regretted her choice to dine with him. Although he was mannerly, he wasn't the least bit interesting to Charlotte. While he prattled on and on about his hobbies and various businesses, all successful according to him, her thoughts drifted to Max. Max hadn't mentioned what he did for a living, and Charlotte hadn't bothered to ask, which she regretted. Max didn't know much about her either, other than the look of her body in scant clothing and the lash of her sharp tongue. She regretted that too.

Simon interrupted her thoughts. "Miss Rose, are you quite well? You seem distracted."

Charlotte started out of her musing. "Pardon me, Mr. Evans. I have a bit of a headache." It was the truth, actually, and the sound of his plummy voice wasn't helping. She recalled how deep and soothing Max's voice sounded.

Simon stood. "Perhaps we should meet another time, my dear. I wish you to be well when we dine." He gave a bow, then pivoted and exited the dining room.

Charlotte watched his retreat. Although he hadn't said anything untoward, and in fact had addressed her in a very polite manner, she felt uneasy about how he took his leave. She realized it wasn't anything he'd said that bothered her, it was what he hadn't said. He hadn't inquired about her health after she admitted a headache, and he seemed irritated, without saying so out loud. Charlotte shrugged to herself and poured another cup of tea, grateful for the time to be alone with her thoughts.

Upon finishing her meal, she walked to the schoolhouse. Max filled her thoughts during her walk just like he had during her breakfast. She felt frustrated and attempted to think badly of him so she could remove him from her mind. She conjured up every infuriating thing about him, from how he insisted on calling her Charlie to how he threatened her with a spanking. Though she didn't succeed in removing him from her mind, she did somewhat succeed in thinking on him negatively for the time being.

Pushing the heavy door to the one-room schoolhouse open with a shove, she entered and got to work cleaning where she'd left off the previous day. Classes would start in two weeks, and the schoolhouse wasn't yet sufficiently prepared. The large room contained two rows of four benches with tables. Each bench would seat up to five children, which, from what she understood of Porter's population, would be sufficient. However, the desks were in a state of terrible disrepair. The legs were cracked and some even broken, and the surfaces of the tables were splintered and showed water damage. Her own desk in the front was missing all of its drawers.

Charlotte sank to her hands and knees to scrub the floor. Though the labor was far from glamorous, she enjoyed it. She was making her own path in life. She felt proud to be a government employee. The schoolhouse was under her care, and she felt a sense of duty and the desire to be the best schoolmarm Porter had ever seen, which started with making sure the room was ready by the time the children began their studies.

An idea came to her after a couple of hours of cleaning. She decided that she needed to visit the marshal. As one of the only other government employees in town, the marshal might be able to advise her on obtaining a stipend from the county to pay for repair of the furniture. Inspired by the thought, she set her scrub brush aside, shook the dust from her skirt, and headed for the jailhouse.

Marshal Huntley greeted her when she opened the door to his office. "Hello, Miss Rose. How are you this morning?" he asked, rising from his desk as she walked in.

"Not bad at all, marshal, thank you."

The two sat across from each other. They discussed the warm weather before Charlotte got to her point about how to request funding. He rubbed his chin and frowned thoughtfully. "Didn't the superintendent inform you of your budget? You should have some funding to use on supplies in addition to your salary."

"Really? No, I had no idea."

"It would be in your contract if so. I'm given a share of money to keep the jail in running order, noted in my contract drawn up by the county sheriff. I assume it would be the same for you."

"I see. Do you know who in town I might hire to repair the schoolhouse furniture?"

"That would be a man you already met— Max Harrison. He can build and repair just about anything."

Charlotte kept the same expression on her face, though her heartbeat quickened and she felt a rush of excitement. "Where might I find him?"

"He owns the blacksmith shop. It's a block east on this street."

"Thank you. I'll go speak to him."

Charlotte rushed out of the jail and took some time to regain her composure. She thought about Max's occupation and smiled to herself. It fit perfectly. He seemed like just the kind of man who could fix and build things. She walked east until she arrived at his shop. A part of her thrilled at the excuse to see him again, but another part of her felt disappointed. She would have preferred that he call upon her, as opposed to the other way around.

Taking a deep breath and squaring her shoulders, she pushed open the door and walked inside, only to discover that the large room was empty of people. Dim light streamed in from the small windows and lit the sparse furniture of the room. The ground was hard concrete that looked recently swept, and a metallic, smoky scent filled the air. Tools hung in neat, straight lines along the walls, and a furnace roared in the center of the room. Curious, she walked to the forge. Next to it stood a metal work table, which held a strip of bent iron. She reached out to pick it up but froze when she heard a familiar voice address her sharply.

"Hold it right there!"

She looked up to find Max striding toward

her from the direction of the open door. He wore buckskin gloves, leather chaps streaked with black stains, and a scowl. She dropped her hand to her side and stared at him as he approached. She swallowed. He looked fiercer and more handsome than she remembered.

He stopped and towered over her, his hands on his hips. "What in the tarnation are you doing? Were you going to touch that iron?"

She stood taller and met his stern gaze, tilting her head higher than what was comfortable to do so. "Good morning to you too, Mr. Harrison."

Groaning, he looked up to the ceiling and ran a hand around his face before looking at her again. "Good morning, Charlie. I thought you were about to grab metal that's a couple hundred degrees, thus my abrupt greeting, but I'm sure I was mistaken. No one could be that foolish, so please excuse my shoddy manners."

She glared at him, stung by his sarcasm and not about to admit her mistake. "It's not a problem, Mr. Harrison. I'm well accustomed to excusing your shoddy manners."

His lips quirked up and his eyes took on a glimmer of amusement. "I see you're just as agreeable as ever."

"I know you speak sarcastically, but I'll have you know I can be quite agreeable. Trouble is, you don't bring it out in me. I don't know how to be friendly when I'm constantly scolded and insulted in your presence."

"Poppycock! I will admit to the scolding. You could use a scolding and a darn good spanking to make sure it's heeded. I don't believe I've ever insulted you though."

Charlotte flushed at his mention of spanking her, and her stomach fluttered. The image of the strong, handsome man taking her in hand suddenly made her legs feel weak, and she thought she might lose her composure.

"And I don't believe I should have come here," she snapped, stepping lightly around his imposing figure. She walked toward the door with a heavy heart. It was clear he didn't wish to see her and thought of her as little more than a fool and nuisance. It hurt her feelings more than she cared to admit, and she wished to lick her wounds in private. Before she reached the door, however, he addressed her in a weary, irritated drawl, as though she were wildly overreacting to his comment.

"Fly your ruffled feathers back here, Charlie."

She stopped and almost stomped her foot in frustration. He was so impertinent, ordering her around and using that horrid nickname for her. She didn't know why she felt any desire to be around him. She turned and glowered at him.

"You must've had a reason for coming. I'd like to know what it is. Come here and talk to me. I'll be nice."

Charlotte suddenly remembered why she'd

come, so she sighed and trudged back. He led her to a bench, where he motioned for her to sit and then sat next to her. His leg brushed her knee, and she felt a shock of arousal travel upward from his accidental touch. Her breath hitched. No man had ever had this effect on her, and she didn't know why her traitorous body had chosen such an infuriating man to be attracted to. She looked over at him, feeling shy suddenly and worried that the way she felt might be obvious to him. She didn't think she could bear it if so. What if he mocked her? Relief came over her when she saw that his expression was kind and encouraging. She took a deep breath and told him why she'd come.

"The desk benches and tables in the schoolhouse are broken down and need to be repaired. I imagine some should even be replaced. The marshal said you were the person to see about this. There's some money from the county to pay you, but I'm not sure how much. I have to read my contract again."

He smiled broadly. "I'd be happy to help. Will you allow me to escort you to the schoolhouse so you can show me what needs doing?"

"All right," she said, standing.

A boy entered as they walked toward the door. He was about Charlotte's height and of slight build. Blond hair draped his forehead and shaded his eyes until he swept it away with the back of his hand.

Max introduced them. "Jim, meet Miss Rose.

She's the new schoolmarm. Miss Rose, this is Jim. He's been my apprentice for some time and also in my care."

Jim blushed a little as he regarded her. He shyly shook the hand Charlotte offered him. "Pleased to meet you, ma'am."

"And you also, Jim. Will I see you in class in a couple of weeks?"

Jim shook his head. "No, ma'am, I've not gone to school for some time now. I like to read, though."

She smiled. "I have a few books I'd be happy to lend to you if you'd like some new material. One is about a boy a few years younger than you who goes on adventures. It's called *Huckleberry Finn*. Does that sound interesting?"

His eyes lit up. "I'd sure as a gun like that. Thank you, Miss Rose."

Charlotte caught Max smiling at her before he turned his attention to the boy. "We've got us a new job, son. Miss Rose is going to show me some desks that need fixing. I'll be back shortly. Get going on smithing a length of chain about the width of my thumb if you don't mind."

"Will do, Max," he said, and walked to the furnace.

Max took off his work gloves and untied the heavy chaps from his trousers, then draped them over a wooden chair against the wall. He washed his hands in a bucket of water near the door of the shop, clapped his Stetson over his head, and held the door open for Charlotte. She passed, and he stepped out behind her.

CHAPTER FOUR

"How are you getting on so far in Porter?" Max inquired as they walked side by side along the wooden sidewalk to the schoolhouse.

"Fine, thank you." She didn't elaborate, and an uncomfortable silence followed. Only the sound of their steps gave away the presence of one to the other.

Finally Max spoke. "Something wrong, Charlie? You seem awful quiet. Did I do something to upset you, other than being my usual loutish self?"

"No, not really," she said, unable to hide the disappointment in her voice.

He stopped and touched her arm to halt her steps. "I'm not an expert on women's feelings, but I'm pretty sure your tone suggests I did. What have I done to vex you?"

Charlotte hesitated, not sure if she should be frank, but then decided it couldn't hurt anything but her pride, which had already been smashed to smithereens in front of him. She sighed and looked at the ground. Her voice was smaller than usual. "I thought you might have inquired about how I was doing before now is all."

She looked up to see his eyebrows lift in surprise. "You mean you wanted me to call on you?"

"It would have been nice," she responded ruefully, looking away again and focusing very hard on a patch of dirt. "But only if you wanted to. It doesn't really matter since you didn't."

"I did want to. Very much," he said quietly, with regret in his voice. "Forgive me. I thought you wouldn't want to see me. But trust me, Charlie, I've all but nailed my feet to the floor to prevent them from running to your doorstep. I've had a devil of a time getting you out of my head."

Charlotte felt her heart swell at his words. She smiled at him. Her smile brought one from him, and they stood in the middle of the sidewalk smiling at each other without speaking for a spell longer than what would be considered normal.

Max broke the silence. "Charlie," he said with resolute force. "I've a mind to take you to lunch and have a good yammer, if that thought doesn't offend you terribly."

She momentarily forgave his impertinent nickname for her. Not only did he care about how she was doing, he fancied spending time with her, which was exactly what she wanted, though she hadn't admitted it to herself until that moment. She blushed and looked down at the dusty sidewalk, then back into his eyes, which were twinkling and hadn't stopped studying her face.

"I admit the prospect of dining with you is not entirely displeasing to me."

Max threw back his head and laughed, holding his hand on the top of his hat to prevent it from falling off. "I feel like that's the best compliment I've ever received. Come along, Miss Rose." He held out a bent arm. "Show me your desks that need fixing. Then I'll take you to lunch before we both get back to work." Charlotte smiled at him again and hooked her hand in the crook of his elbow.

Max examined the furniture in the schoolhouse and pointed out where some of the wood had rotted. He explained that there must be a leak in the roof that allowed rain to soak into a good number of desks, causing them to become brittle and likely to break sooner rather than later. Charlotte's desk needed drawers, which he explained would require measuring and crafting pieces fitted with metal sliders.

Max shook his head. "This furniture is in a sorry state. I can't help but wonder why the previous schoolteacher didn't hire me."

"Will it require a great deal of your time?" Charlotte asked.

"Yes, but it must be done. Even a small child's weight could break some of these benches.

I'll get started on it tomorrow. Hopefully I can finish before your classes start."

"That's awfully good news, Max. As soon as I read my contract and determine the amount available, I'll withdraw the funds to give to you."

"You called me Max. Thank you." He winked at her.

"You could thank me by not calling me Charlie."

Max laughed. "I'll try not to, but I make no promises. How about we get some chow? I'm feeling wolfish." He held his arm out again. She latched on and they walked the few blocks to Mary's Diner.

Once they were seated and had each been served their meal, he said, "I've been curious about something. What made you leave home and come all the way out here?"

Charlotte swallowed her bite of mashed potatoes, which were tolerable and had only a few lumps in them. "I wanted adventure, and I wanted to use my education. I was uninterested in becoming a wife and mother right away. Not that I don't want children. I do," she added hastily, then blushed, realizing her last statement was unnecessary.

"Me too. I've always liked children and thought I'd be raising a few long before now," he said in a matter-of-fact manner. "Go on. What else rattled your hocks all the way here?"

Something about the way he spoke to her, in

such a plain way without airs or devices, caused her to be forthright as well. "To be frank, I didn't want to lead the life my mother led, married to my father, who never loved her or me. I felt afraid of that. I was courted by multiple men who seemed just like my father, and I guess I felt I needed to get away and see what else the world had to offer."

Max cocked his head and frowned at her. "How could your father not love you?"

She shrugged. "He doesn't think much of women in general, I suppose. Growing up, I heard him call my mother ugly and stupid or some variation of that every chance he got. My mother was able to protect me from his insults and scorn most of the time, but I didn't always escape it."

Max shook his head. "No wonder you're so...." His voice trailed off.

Charlotte stiffened. "So what?" she demanded.

He smiled at her without mockery. "Defensive."

Charlotte's shoulders slumped. "I shouldn't have been so upfront. I've never told anyone of my troubles with my father. I don't know why I burdened you."

Max set his fork down and reached across the table to cover her hand with his, causing her to look into his eyes. "I'm glad you told me, Charlie. I want to know you better. I took a shine to you the moment you first sassed me on the station's platform, and the way I felt got stronger the more time I spent with you."

Charlotte felt warmed by his touch and his words. She couldn't believe how easily he told her that. "Really?" she asked, peering at him through her lashes.

"Don't feign surprise," he admonished with a smile, removing his hand. He picked up his fork and knife and sliced into the roast beef on his plate. "You must know I'm one of many men who would give up five Sundays for five minutes of your company."

"I'm not feigning surprise, Max. I really do feel surprised. I know many men find me attractive, but you didn't seem to like me much. I suppose I couldn't blame you if you didn't. I acted a bit spoiled on our first meeting."

Max snorted. "A bit?" He ate a bite of roast beef and leaned back in his chair. His eyes twinkled as he chewed and waited for her reaction.

For once, Charlotte didn't react with outrage at his needling. "You like drawing my ire, don't you? You're worse than a schoolboy who likes a girl and shows it by pulling her hair."

He leaned forward and drank some water. "That's probably true. I'd like to show you how I feel in nicer ways though, Charlotte." He spoke in a low voice that held promise.

She felt her cheeks grow warm at his forward remark and the smooth way her name rolled off his tongue. She concentrated on buttering her roll. "Enough about me. I'm curious about you. Have you ever been married?"

"Yes, more than ten years ago. But it ended in divorce."

"Really? That's unusual."

"Mm hmm, and unfortunate. Like you, she was from the east. She came all the way from New York but went back within a year of marrying me. It was too rough out here for her, and I was too stubborn and selfish to show any kind of understanding. If I had, it might have given her cause to stay."

"It's big of you to admit that," Charlotte said, impressed by his humility and willingness to share his regret with her.

"I'm older and wiser now." He gave her a pointed look. "I won't make the same mistake. If I marry again, I will ensure my wife's happiness."

Charlotte looked down, unused to a man so openly explaining what kind of husband he intended to be. Max didn't have a lick of guile or artfulness. She found it refreshing, but it also made her feel exposed and vulnerable. It seemed he knew the unspoken questions she had about him.

She changed the subject. "How long has Jim been your apprentice?"

"Going on two years now, but he's more than an apprentice. He's like a son to me."

"Oh? Why's that?"

Max hesitated for a beat, but then explained. "Like you, he doesn't have a particularly pleasant father. That became clear to me when he showed up to work every day with fear in his eyes and fresh bruises."

Charlotte gasped. "Poor child. That's awful."

"I thought so too, which is why I convinced his father to let him stay with me. Jim is doing better now. He's still very shy. That might never change, and I reckon it's all right if it doesn't. He's a good lad."

She smiled. "Careful, Max. I'm beginning to think you're a nice man."

He grinned back at her. "Well, we can't have that."

"No," she agreed, and picked up her saucer and teacup. She sipped her tea daintily.

"I'm not too worried though. I have a feeling your impertinence will often bring out a side of me that's distinctly not nice."

She set her tea on the table. The china rattled. "You think *I'm* impertinent? This coming from the most impertinent man I know?"

"I guess we make a good pair," he said, leaning back and chuckling.

"Is that what we are, Max? A pair?" she inquired with a shy smile, hoping he would confirm it.

Before he could answer, however, Simon Evans appeared next to their table. Charlotte noticed his clothing for the first time. In Boston, he would have fit right in with his well-pressed trousers and silk brown vest over a starched white shirt. He held in his hand a clean hat that matched the color of his vest. In Porter, he looked fancier than every other man, much as Charlotte did every other woman.

"Hello again, Max," he said.

The smile left Max's face. He nodded curtly. "Simon."

Charlotte felt herself tense up when the man turned his attention to her.

"And hello again to you, Miss Rose. I gather your illness was not long-lasting. I see you feel well enough to entertain a new gentleman only hours after your first. I'm most pleased by your speedy recovery."

Charlotte felt like she'd been caught doing something wrong, and she felt embarrassed by his words, which made her sound like she made a habit of spending time with multiple men. She glanced at Max.

"You were unwell?" Max asked, scrunching his brows together.

"Yes. I mean no—I had a headache," she finished lamely.

Max observed her with an unreadable expression.

She sat a little straighter and tried to sound unruffled. "My head feels better. Thank you for asking, Mr. Evans."

"My pleasure, dear. We can't have the prettiest woman in all of Porter unwell. How else will all the men you see find satisfaction?" He flashed a perfect white smile at her, which didn't reach his eyes.

Charlotte looked down at her plate and blinked, humiliated by the thinly veiled insult. She wouldn't have minded so much if he'd said it just for her ears, and she probably would have battled it out and set the man straight if he had. Max's presence, however, rendered her speechless and distraught. She feared what he might think of her, and her cheeks burned.

Max stood from the table abruptly, his chair scraping loudly across the floor as he did. "Are you finished with your meal, Miss Rose?" His voice sounded angry, which made Charlotte's spirits sink lower. He must be displeased with her.

She nodded and stood as well, her eyes cast downward.

Max addressed Simon, his voice hard as steel, without the lilt of false cordiality used by the other man. "If you need a table to sit at, you can use this one. We're leaving."

"Thank you, Max. How very generous," Simon said with a sneer.

Max stepped around him and took Charlotte's elbow. He led her away from the table without another word and strode to the front of the restaurant. He released her arm to pay the bill, thanked the waitress, and then held her arm again. He only let go of her when they were alone inside the schoolhouse. That's when he spoke, his voice heavy with disapproval.

CHAPTER FIVE

"**C**harlie, have you become friendly with Simon Evans?"

Charlotte shook her head emphatically. "No, Max, not in any way other than polite. He stays at the same boardinghouse as I do. He invited me to breakfast this morning and I accepted. I had a headache, though, and he left before the meal's end." She looked pleadingly into Max's eyes, which flashed with fury. "Please don't think ill of me. I don't make it a habit to dine with two men in one day. He made me seem like a loose woman. I'm not, I assure you."

His expression softened slightly. "Of course you're not, Charlie. I don't think ill of you. I think ill of him. He's a cruel man. Listen carefully to what I say now. You're not to dine with him again or spend any time alone with him. Is that understood?"

Charlotte flinched, and her temper flared. She suddenly remembered why Max always managed to irritate her. "Max, what right do you have to order me about? I'm a grown woman, perfectly capable of deciding whether I wish to spend time with someone, and I'll thank you not to boss me. It galls me."

Max raised his voice. "That's too damn bad, young lady. You will mind my words. I speak them for your safety, not for your pleasure. As for the right to give you orders, I want you to be my woman, and unless I'm really bad at reading signals, you want that too." He held a finger to her face. "If you want me to court you, Charlotte Rose, you must agree to obey me."

Charlotte stared at him and then stammered her response. "That was the worst offer of courtship in the history of courtships."

"That could very well be," he growled. "But I'm not concerned about being courtly at the moment. I'm concerned about your stubborn pride getting in the way of your safety. Look here, Charlie. Whether or not you want me to court you, I insist you stay away from him or else answer to me. I won't watch you harmed at that man's hands, and I'll do whatever needs doing to prevent it. Have I made myself clear?"

Charlotte looked into his fierce eyes and swallowed hard. She felt something blooming inside of her that she'd never felt before. It grew stronger than her irritation. It was a feeling of gratefulness and trust. For the first time, she felt like a man cared enough to protect her, and not just any man, a man she believed capable of doing so. What all but eliminated her annoyance was learning than he would ensure her safety even if she offered him nothing in return.

"Yes, sir. It's clear," she said, lowering her eyes to the floor.

"You agree to stay away from him then, Charlotte?"

"Yes, Max," she said, her eyes still cast downward.

"Good girl."

His two simple words caused her new feeling to grow, as though what bloomed inside of her had been sprinkled with rain.

"Have I mentioned yet that Simon is Jim's father?"

Charlotte's head shot up. "No."

"Right. Now you know. That's the man who beats his own son, and he punches women as easily as he bows to them." Max removed his intense gaze from her face. He walked to a bench that had escaped water damage, sat down, and held out his hand. "Come here, Charlotte, and place yourself over my lap. I'm going to give you that spanking I've mentioned a couple of times."

Charlotte's mouth fell open, and her stomach tightened into knots. A few beats passed before she found her voice, which was small and pleading. "But Max, I promised I wouldn't see him again. I told you I would mind your words."

"Yes, and for that reason, I don't plan to

be too hard on you. However, you only agreed after giving me lip and reminding me about your stubborn pride. It's what led to you becoming ill from heatstroke, and I believe it could lead to much worse if I don't address it. Come to me now, or it'll be a longer punishment."

The expression on his face left no room for argument. Charlotte thought she'd never seen a man so intent on doing something as Max seemed intent on spanking her. She felt her feet walk in his direction as her mind spun. She'd never been subjected to any form of corporal punishment, and she hated the thought of being spanked by a man she very much wanted to remain dignified around. It seemed dignity wasn't an option when it came to Max, who had already seen her in various states of upheaval. Her lips formed into a pout as she reached out her hand to him. His warm, callused fingers enclosed her soft hand, and he guided her smoothly over his lap.

"Good girl," he said again, and Charlotte felt relieved that he didn't seem angry with her. He lifted her skirt and positioned it on her back. "On our journey from Arcadia together, I could tell it hurt your feelings when I threatened a spanking, but I only did so because it scared me when you became ill, and I felt angry when you didn't seem to pay it any mind. I didn't want to make you feel sad. Do you understand that now?"

"Yes," she said meekly, as he pushed up one of her two petticoats.

"The last thing I want is to break your spirit. I don't want to change who you are, Charlotte. I find your cheek and smart mouth quite adorable, to be honest, but when it comes to health and safety, I don't wish to hear your tart replies or arguments. I want you to listen to what I say and obey it."

He lifted her other petticoat. Only her thin drawers protected her tender seat. He settled his hand on her bottom, and she felt the same current of arousal she'd experienced earlier in the day when his thigh touched her knee, only this time the feeling was much, much stronger.

He gave her seat a few light pats and rubs. "Ten swats, Charlotte."

The rubs heightened her arousal, but it was quickly replaced by alarm when he inflicted a punishing swat on her right cheek. She gasped with surprise. Before she could exhale, he landed another on her left. The emptiness of the schoolhouse allowed the swats' echoes to ring in her ears as the sting spread over her bottom.

The next three slaps fell briskly. His large hand covered both cheeks at once, landing low on her bottom and in the same place, and Charlotte yelped and felt her eyes fill with tears. She had never felt so small and helpless, nor had she felt so much of a man's focused attention, as she did at that moment over Max's lap.

"Halfway done," he murmured, rubbing her bottom in circles, relieving some of the sting. She sniffled, and his hand stopped rubbing when he heard her.

"This is mild discipline, Charlotte, only a few swats to get your attention and let you know I mean business, and it sounds like you're crying. It's not really that bad, is it?"

"N-no, I guess not. But I've never been spanked."

He resumed rubbing. "I didn't think so. A man's firm care is new to you. This is one of the less pleasant aspects of it, but I think you'll find it preferable to someone not caring enough to do it. How old are you?"

"Twenty-four."

"Mm hmm, that's about what I thought. I've got a whole decade on you, darlin'." His hand connected again smartly with the low curve of her left cheek. "That's ten more years of experience in this world and thirty-four more in this part of it."

He landed another swat on her right cheek. "So the way I see it, if in the future I suggest changing into different clothing, I will expect you to do so without argument because I know the weather here. Is that fair, Charlotte?"

"Yes, sir."

"And if I order you to avoid someone for your own safety, I expect you to be agreeable to it without giving me attitude because I know the people here. Is that fair as well?"

Charlotte spoke quietly. "Yes, Max. I want to obey you, and I want you to court me."

"I'm happy to hear that, sweetheart. I very much want to court you too. Three more swats, and then I'm going to give you a big hug. Will I ever have to spank you again for allowing stubborn pride to affect your health and safety?"

"No, I will listen to you."

"And make good choices on your own?"

"Yes, sir."

"Good girl. If I must spank you again for this, I won't be lenient. All right, Charlotte?"

"All right, Max," she said, and closed her eyes, bracing herself for the pain that would come from the last of the punishment.

His hand fell smartly in succession, which stung, but in general the punishment hadn't been as awful as she imagined it might be. He carefully straightened her petticoats and dress back over her backside. She felt a new warmth toward Max. He had seen past her defenses and rebellion and located something inside of her she didn't know she had—a desire to be taken care of.

"Thank you, Max."

Max helped her stand and immediately brought her to sit on his lap. He enclosed her in the promised hug. "For what, darlin'? Spanking you?"

"I guess, and for caring. I just... I feel grateful for how I feel right now. I feel vulnerable, but not scared. I don't know how to explain it."

Max loosened his grip and leaned back to study her wet eyes for a moment, then wrapped her up in his arms again. He sighed. "Oh, honey.

What you just described sounds an awful lot like the feeling of being loved. You haven't had much of that, have you? No matter, I intend to make up for it plenty."

She leaned her head against his chest and listened to his heartbeat. Time passed during which they said nothing and only felt the presence and touch of the other. Charlotte lifted her head after some time and looked deeply into his green eyes. Max smiled. She thought he might kiss her. She could almost see it cross his mind, but instead he stood up, bringing her to her feet as well.

"I've got to get back to work. Would you like me to escort you home first?"

Charlotte shook her head. "No, thank you. I'm going to continue cleaning and then write some lesson plans."

"What time are you leaving?"

"Oh, I don't know. After I feel I've made good progress, I suppose."

Max gave her a peck on the cheek, then turned and headed for the door. "The sun sets around six o'clock. Make sure you're home before then. Unfortunately it's not safe for a lady to walk around alone here after dark."

Charlotte smiled. Before the spanking, she would have felt irritated about being told to go home before dark, but now she only felt grateful for Max's care.

Max pulled the door to the schoolhouse open and looked back at her. "Bye, darlin'. I'll come find you tomorrow and take you to lunch. It'll only be for a quick meal though. I'm terribly busy with work."

"And now you're even busier," Charlotte said, waving her hand in the direction of the decrepit furniture.

"Yes, but that's one job I look forward to doing, as I hope to please you." He winked and disappeared out the door.

CHAPTER SIX

Max walked with a light step from the schoolhouse to his shop. He felt a few inches taller than before his time with Charlotte. He whistled a tune and thought out a plan to fix the schoolhouse's furniture. He owned enough raw wood to replace the rotted benches, so that would be easy enough. He would work on that first and finish them before classes started so that no child would be in danger of breaking a seat and falling. The tables could be done later, if necessary. To prevent future wood rot, he and Jim would also need to patch any leaks in the roof upon discovering where they came from during the next rainfall.

Max heard a thud coming from inside his shop as he neared. He stopped whistling, which allowed him to hear a loud voice he recognized. Clenching his jaw, he walked to the door and shoved it open. He was greeted by the sight of Simon launching a hammer at Jim, followed by Jim ducking in time for the tool to hit the wall behind him.

Anger surged through Max, and his voice boomed. "Simon, what the hell are you doing in my shop throwing around my tools?" He strode in his direction, fury making him feel like a powerful giant. "You all right, Jim?" he asked as he walked toward the man.

"Yeah. His aim has gotten worse," Jim replied. His voice sounded dry and numb with hatred.

Max stopped in front of Simon, who stood up straighter and appeared to be gathering his wits. It took every ounce of self-control for Max not to punch him when he smiled.

"Do forgive me, Max. My son and I were having a bit of a disagreement."

Max gritted his teeth at how he referred to Jim as his son, which as far as Max was concerned, he had no business doing, having never treated him like one. "You're welcome to disagree with Jim, but not in my shop when he's supposed to be working, and not with violence. What's this all about?" Max glanced at the boy, who stood on the other side of the room with his arms crossed and his eyes set on his father. Something had changed in his posture. He didn't appear afraid, only disgusted and angry.

"I hope you didn't just tell me how to raise my own son," Simon said jovially. "While I admit your shop is not the ideal location, and I do apologize, how I treat my son is none of your concern."

"Tell me what this is about," Max growled, impatient to deal with it so he could be rid of the man.

"Once again, it's none of your concern," Simon responded. He fixed Jim with a hard stare before he strutted out the door.

Max tossed his Stetson on a chair and looked at the boy, who avoided meeting his eyes. He sat on his bench to resume his task of forming a chain.

"Well, Jim?"

"It's nothing," the boy responded, not looking up from his work.

"Bosh!" Max exclaimed. "Something is wrong, and you know very well I won't let it go that easy. Now you stop what you're doing and start exercising your jaw."

Jim kept the chain in his hand and looked at him. "I don't want to discuss it, Max," he said, quietly and with resolve.

Max stared at him for a moment, dumbfounded, and then cleared his throat. "Now you look here, young man. I'm proud of you for having the courage to stand your ground, but I'm disappointed that it's happening now and with me. You've been secretive lately, and I thought I'd earned your trust."

Jim looked down at the chain and shook his head. "I do trust you, Max. It has nothing to do with trust. I'm my own man, and I can take care of this situation."

Max tied the strings of his chaps around his waist with a yank, then stuffed his gloves over his hands. "Unbelievable," he muttered as he strode to his work table. He felt exasperated and offended that Jim and Simon shared knowledge of something without his involvement, and he didn't like that whatever it was led to violence against the boy.

He swept metal shards off his table and pondered Jim's unusual words and behavior, such as claiming to be his own man. Max let out an irritated sigh. Jim was still a boy, a vulnerable one at that, and he seemed to be in need of a man's help. Max would help him without question, if Jim would only tell him how he might. Max worried silently, and the two of them didn't speak again until Jim prepared to leave.

"I finished the chain. Thanks for letting me go early, Max."

"It's all right, Jim," he said without looking up from his task, which was drafting the dimensions and structure for the benches.

Max didn't hear him leave. He looked over and found the boy observing him with a pained expression. Max set his pencil on the table as Jim approached. Jim didn't stop until he'd reached Max and wrapped his arms around him. Max felt stunned for a moment, but then returned the hug with a tight squeeze. He only released him when he felt the boy's arms soften their grip around his waist. Max tousled his hair and gave him a small shove.

"Get out of here, scamp, before I give you a licking."

Jim offered him a small smile that held love and sorrow. He knew by then that Max wouldn't lay a finger on him after the abuse he'd endured from his father. Maybe if Max were his real father, he might have suffered a walloping or two growing up, but not the kind that would have left him bruised and bloody. Both Max and Jim wished the past was different and that the other was in it.

After Jim left, Max tried to figure out what the boy could possibly be up to that he didn't feel comfortable sharing with him. He considered trying to coax the information from Simon, but that idea was even more distasteful to him than remaining ignorant. The situation rankled him, but he decided to honor Jim's wish to keep the information private. He worked to push it out of his mind and mostly succeeded, since his thoughts were easily filled with Charlotte and his mounting work.

*　*　*

Jim trudged along the sidewalk toward the telegraph office a few blocks from the shop, his slow steps reflecting the dread he felt about carrying out his errand. He needed to send an answer to New York regarding the college scholarship he'd been offered. The words of the telegram would either be in obedience to his father or in direct opposition, and he hadn't yet decided which message to send.

He tensed and clenched his jaw, thinking about Simon. He feared his father and had done so since he was old enough to feel fear, and he hated him from the same age. His memories of childhood contained little else but violence and, in the absence of that, the unrelenting threat of it. His only relief from the pain and chaos was the time he spent reading alone, during which he could escape the reality of his life.

His father put up a good front in public most of the time, charming those he met with his eloquence and gentlemanly manners. While his wife and son had struggled to survive off the paltry earnings he brought home, Simon remained well-dressed, well-fed, and well-entertained as a regular at the saloon. As Jim grew older, so did his awareness of his father's cruel neglect, but he never stood up to him, knowing that if he did, the repercussions would be severe.

Jim didn't think much of his mother either. Although he never feared her, he viewed her as selfish and uncaring. She did nothing to protect him from his father, and she eventually abandoned him to suffer the man alone. Things only got worse after his mother left, about a year before Jim became Max's apprentice. During that time, all of Simon's rage focused on Jim, who reminded Simon of his wife and his failure as a husband.

Jim's thoughts wandered to Max, and he felt a painful constriction in his chest. Nearly two years ago, after reading about apprenticeship in one of the novels he borrowed, Jim set out on the town, intent on learning a trade, any trade that would provide him with enough financial support to leave his father and live on his own when he came of age. It took every ounce of courage for him to walk into the blacksmith's shop. He recalled the words he exchanged with Max that day. His voice shook, and he felt like his very life depended on Max saying yes to his request. Perhaps, in hindsight, it did.

"Mr. Harrison, I'm interested in learning a trade, and I wonder if I might offer my labor in exchange for your knowledge. I would be a diligent and obedient apprentice."

Max regarded him with a confused expression. "I never really thought about taking on an apprentice, Jim. What makes you interested in blacksmithing? I always thought your father had greater plans for you."

At the time, Max didn't know the truth behind closed doors at Jim's house, only the front Simon presented of himself being a highly educated man with a son who invariably scored high marks in school.

"My father is agreeable to me smithing. I've

already asked, so you don't need to," Jim lied, desperation creeping into his words.

Max frowned at his response, and he didn't agree to take him as an apprentice right away. When Jim showed up the next day, Max directed his attention to the wall of the shop. On it hung more than twenty-five tools of the trade. Max pointed at each tool and gave its name in addition to its use. When he finished speaking after some time, he asked Jim to tell him what he'd just learned.

Jim repeated the information nearly word for word, and Max's eyes grew wide in amazement. "Sakes alive, Jim. I expected you to remember some of what I said, but you remembered everything. I reckon I'd be lucky to have you as an apprentice, though your memory might be better suited for a higher purpose."

Jim felt afraid to get his hopes up. "Does that mean I can work for you, Mr. Harrison?"

"Yes. I will just need to speak with your father first, to make sure this arrangement is all right with him."

Jim's spirits sank upon hearing those words, which must have reflected in his face and posture because Max rubbed the beard on his chin and said, "I think I can convince Simon, don't worry."

Max did convince Simon after some negotiating, the specifics of which Jim didn't learn until later. Jim dropped out of school immediately and began work, showing up on his first day with a black eye. Max said nothing about the bruise and put him to work manning the forge right away. He told Jim to keep it supplied with coal and not let the fire go out. Jim's hands shook, terrified of making a mistake, and he let the fire die when he became distracted watching Max hammer iron over the anvil.

Max approached him when he noticed the lack of fire, and Jim shrank back, equally afraid of being punished and of being fired. "Now, Jim," Max chided. "Keep focus on the task I gave you. When you prove you can do that, I'll give you a more interesting one."

Jim nodded and felt relief when Max tousled his hair and returned to his work station. It was the first of Jim's many mistakes, all of which Max reacted mildly to, and with humor occasionally. Once he laughed when Jim melted a strip of iron to liquid that couldn't be shaped or salvaged after it mixed with the ashes in the forge. Jim felt horrified, but Max said, "You'll get the hang of it. I'm only laughing because I remember doing that myself as a boy. My father was fit to be tied, but I escaped a thrashing. He swore like the dickens and scolded me for an hour after, but he was a forgiving man beneath his brusque exterior."

"Much like you," Jim dared to say.

Max smiled. "Maybe so. I reckon there are worse things to be compared to than my father, God rest his soul."

Jim looked down. "I hope I am never

compared to my father." When he looked up, all mirth had disappeared from Max's eyes, replaced by a spark of anger.

"I'm sorry, Jim. I've had my suspicions of his treatment of you, but I wasn't sure."

Jim shrugged and turned his attention to cleaning up the mess he'd made. The next day, Max informed Jim that he'd spoken with his father and arranged for Jim to live with him, if he so wished. Jim felt surprised, then overjoyed. The day he moved in with Max was the day his life became something worth living.

Nearly two years later, as Jim walked to the telegraph office, he realized that his love for Max far outweighed his fear of his father. He came to a halt and leaned against a hitching post. Covering his forehead with his hand, he thought hard about which telegram would work better in Max's favor. He shook his head, feeling great distress and confusion. He couldn't decide, so he didn't send either. He turned away from his errand and walked home.

* * *

Charlotte was in love. Every hardship and annoyance slid off her back like ice off a hot plate. She wrote to her mother and gushed about her new beau and all the wonderful things he said and did. She left out the spanking, of course, though it was in the forefront of her mind. She sat at her desk in her room at the boardinghouse and gazed out the window, recalling the discipline over Max's lap. She decided she wouldn't like a spanking much harder than what she'd received, but she liked how it made her feel, especially when Max held her in his arms and comforted her afterwards. The spanking had made her feel soft and vulnerable and, as a result, able to enjoy the full benefit of Max's strong and tender care. She overflowed with a sense of well-being like she'd never experienced before.

Max took her to dinner nearly every evening, despite his long work hours. She felt guilty that the task of quickly building and repairing the schoolhouse furniture, along with keeping up with his other work, caused him fatigue, but she comforted herself by knowing he would be paid by the county. She still awaited word from Dallas regarding the exact sum available. She'd read her contract again, which made no mention of funding, so she wired the superintendent requesting information and payment. She was impatient to receive the money to hand to Max.

A little more than a week after they began courting, Charlotte set out toward Max's house on a cool Sunday morning, carrying the book she'd promised Jim. Birds chirped around her, adding a spring to her already light step on the dirt path. Max's house was about a half-mile outside of town, so it was an easy, pleasant walk.

Shortly after the start of her journey, she heard the sound of raised voices ahead. When she rounded the corner and saw who they came from, she stopped. Jim and Simon stood in the middle of the road, engaged in a heated argument.

"I'm not going anywhere, Simon," Jim said to his father. "I want to stay with Max and continue working for him."

Simon held a shaking fist up to the boy's face. "Are you addled? You have less brains than a headless chicken if you think I'll back down. You are your mother's son."

"Good," Jim replied. "Though I'm about as fortunate in that regard as I am having you as my father. I'm going to stay with Max and remain his employee when I come of age."

"You do that, I'll ruin him. I'll make his life so miserable he'll wish he'd never met you."

Jim's eyes flashed with anger, and his hands closed into fists at his sides. He looked away from his father's face, and that's when he noticed Charlotte. His brow furrowed.

She reluctantly walked in their direction. "I'm sorry to interrupt," Charlotte said meekly, feeling ashamed that she'd eavesdropped and also alarmed by the conversation she'd overheard.

Simon turned around slowly to face her. "Well, if it isn't the charming schoolmarm. How do you do, Miss Rose?" He smiled, but it looked more like a grimace.

"I'm well. I'll be on my way to see Max." She continued walking and passed them.

"*Max*, is it?" Simon sneered. "Are you that familiar with the blacksmith?"

"Yes," Charlotte said simply, stopping with a half turn to look at him. "Max is courting me."

Simon snorted. "Well, isn't he a lucky man? How did he manage to garner your affections? Was it his soot-stained breeches you found attractive? Or perhaps his sweaty pits?"

Charlotte turned around fully to face him. "Perhaps both," she said, with a haughty lift of her chin. "I respect a man who makes an honest living."

Simon laughed without humor, then turned his attention back to his son. "Perhaps you should escort the lady to your master's house. I've said all I need to say. It's your turn to do what needs to be done, and you'd best remember this: I'm quickly running out of patience."

Simon tipped his hat to Charlotte and walked in the direction of town. Jim stared after him for a bit, then sauntered to Charlotte's side. They walked together in silence for some time before Jim said quietly, "How much of my conversation with Simon did you hear, Miss Rose?"

"I'm sorry, Jim. It was terribly rude of me to listen for as long as I did, and I'm afraid I heard enough to alarm me. I heard your father say he would ruin Max. What was that about?"

Jim sighed. "I'm in a bind. I've been trying

for weeks to be shed of it. Normally I would seek Max's advice, but I don't want to with this. I feel lost at sea."

"Perhaps I can help?" Charlotte offered.

Jim didn't say anything, so Charlotte changed the subject. She handed the boy her copy of *Huckleberry Finn*. "Do let me know what you think. I love talking about literature with folks. I hope to find more people in town with a love of reading."

Jim took the book from her. "Thank you." A moment later he added tentatively, "It's my love of reading that got me into this quandary."

Charlotte eyed him with surprise. "How? I've never heard of reading causing problems, only the lack of it."

Jim drew a deep breath. "There's a book club in town. I've been attending for over a year."

"That sounds like good fun," Charlotte said.

"It was, until I got it into my head to take an exam offered by a recruiter who attended. It was to test my readiness for college, which I'd never intended on going to. I took the test for the heck of it, but I ended up scoring very high. Higher than everyone else, and I was offered a scholarship. The first to find out was me, the second was Simon."

"That's impressive, Jim! What did Max say? He must be very proud."

"That's the thing, Miss Rose. He doesn't know, and I don't want him to. I want to stay with Max and be a blacksmith, not go off to some fancy college. Not that it would happen even if I wanted it to. The scholarship money would be placed in the hands of Simon, since I'm not yet eighteen. Simon knows this and has told me he intends to keep it for himself. I wouldn't see a penny."

Charlotte felt surprised that Simon had threatened something so dubious, but also skeptical about its likelihood for success. "The college would know the money had been stolen when you didn't attend. There's no way your father could get away with that."

"He's already figured out a way. If he bullies me into leaving town, he'll be able to say he gave the money to me and I skipped out with it. No one would be suspicious of him."

Charlotte took in a sharp breath and felt angry on the boy's behalf. His own father wanted to frame him for theft. "So, from what I understand, you're refusing to accept the scholarship and leave town, and Simon is angry because that means he won't be paid. But why and how would he hurt Max?"

"Simon knows that the best way to make me do what he says is to threaten harm on the one person I care about. He'd find a way to take away everything Max holds dear." Jim gave Charlotte a sidelong glance. "That might include you, since Max is sweet on you. You should stay away from Simon. He wouldn't think twice about hurting you if it suited his purposes."

Charlotte rubbed her forehead. "Yes, I've

already been warned. I don't know what to say, Jim. There must be a way out of it, surely."

"I keep trying to think of something. The way I see it, either way, Max gets burned. If I do Simon's bidding and leave, Max will lose his apprentice. If I stay and incur Simon's wrath, Max will keep me as his apprentice but might lose a whole lot more."

Max's cabin appeared ahead of them, and the two walked in silence a few paces. Finally Charlotte said, "I'm glad you told me. No one should deal with this kind of problem alone. I will try to think of something."

"Thank you, Miss Rose, but please don't tell Max."

Charlotte sighed. "It's not for me to tell him, but I think you should. He's good at fixing things. He might be able to fix this."

Jim stopped suddenly, bringing Charlotte's steps to a halt as well. "Miss Rose, perhaps I don't need to tell you this, but as tough as Max is, he's also very kind. He wouldn't think twice about sacrificing himself for me. He already has, you know. He's paying Simon for my work, despite also providing my room and board and spending countless hours teaching me everything he knows. He has protected me ever since he knew me, to his detriment. I don't want him to do that in this situation. I won't let Simon win here, and I'm determined to figure out a way out of this so that Max doesn't get the short end of the stick. If I tell

Max, he will set in motion a plan to my benefit, not to his own. He still thinks of me as a child, a child he needs to protect, and I want to be the man here and finally do right by him."

Charlotte listened without interrupting, a lump growing in her throat as she did. The love between Max and Jim was apparent. When she reflected on Max's gentle and protective treatment of the abused boy, she saw that it resembled his care toward her. Jim and Charlotte were also alike in their need to prove something to Max. Jim wanted to prove he was a strong man, not a scared boy, and Charlotte wanted to prove she was a capable woman, not a foolish girl. She fully understood Jim's reticence to involve Max in his troubles.

"I won't tell him, Jim, and I'll help you however I can."

CHAPTER SEVEN

Charlotte's classes began. The children sat on sturdy new benches and wrote on desks without splinters. Max was able to finish all the work before school started. He even surprised Charlotte by building a brand new desk for her using rich mahogany wood. She entered the schoolhouse an hour before the children showed up on the first day. Her eyes immediately fell on the beautiful desk in the front. She ran to it and opened the top drawer, which contained a pink rose and a note.

Good luck on your first day, Miss Rose. I wanted you to have a little something extra. Love, Max

The gesture was practical and sweet, just like Max, and it brought a huge smile to her face that lasted the entire day, which was a difficult one. She learned that most of the children were a couple of years behind in their education and required more attention than she'd thought they would. Still, she enjoyed the work more and more as the days passed, and she adored the children, most of whom were eager to please and studious in their homework.

After a couple of weeks of teaching, she received her first paycheck, which gave her a sense of pride and accomplishment. Sitting at her desk in her room at the boardinghouse, she struggled to write out a spending plan for the next two weeks. Teaching came naturally to Charlotte, but budgeting did not. She chewed her pencil and wrote down each expense she could think of. Her rent at the boardinghouse cost the most, but she would receive another check before the rent was due and so could use her first check to buy food and other necessities. She also had a little money in savings to fall back on.

It was during this budgeting session that she heard a knock at her door. Upon opening it, she found a lad holding a telegram. "From Dallas, miss," the boy said.

Charlotte thanked him and returned to her desk to read it. Her heart sank and her breathing became labored upon reading its contents. It was a message from the superintendent.

Miss Charlotte Rose <stop> *No funding available for school furniture* <stop> *Please make do* <stop> *Thanks for your dedication* <stop> *Superintendent Ed Haskins* <stop>

Charlotte stared at the note for some time, overcome with multiple feelings—anger at the superintendent for denying such a basic need, anger at herself for assuming the need would be met, followed by guilt and embarrassment over asking Max to perform such a large task without verifying the funding to back it up.

She felt terribly foolish. How could she have been so naïve? She imagined the conversation she might have with Max, telling him she'd been wrong about the money. She groaned. She loathed the thought of telling him. Charlotte paced the room, furious at herself and furious at Max too. He would be understanding. He would tell her not to worry about it. But it would be another foolish mistake he'd have against her. Damn him. She knew her anger toward him was illogical, but she worked herself up to such a state of dismay over her error that she became determined to save her pride. Above all else, Max could not know about this.

She came to a decision. Sitting back at her desk, she made hasty calculations and rushed to the bank to exchange her check for money. Following that, she walked to Max's shop. He smiled upon seeing her and set down the metal file he held.

"Hello, darlin'," he drawled.

Jim greeted her from the other side of the room.

Charlotte walked to where Max stood by the forge and handed him the money, all of her income for two weeks of teaching. "I got the money from

Dallas for the furniture today. Is that enough?"

Max rifled through the bills and counted the money. "This is just fine. It pays for all the supplies."

Charlotte let out a breath she hadn't realized she'd been holding. She would use her savings to buy food, and two weeks later when she received her next paycheck, she would pay rent. Max never need know about her foolish mistake. It was a good plan, and she couldn't find fault in it; that is, until the day it shattered into pieces and led to the scariest moment of her life.

* * *

Charlotte's bare feet sprinted along the dirt path, lit only by a sliver of a moon. She inhaled loudly to fill her strangled lungs, bereft of oxygen from exertion and terror. The sounds of her breathing didn't drown out the pounding steps that fell heavily and grew louder as they gained distance behind her. She heard a shriek exit her lips as her feet tripped over her long skirt. She scrambled in a panic to find her balance, realizing that a fall would give her pursuer all the time he needed to catch up. She gathered the calico material into both of her fists and surged ahead, fear masking any pain from the bruises and cuts forming on the bottom of her feet.

She could see Max's house in the distance

and the soft glow of a lamp behind the window. He was awake. All she needed to do was get to him in time. Nothing else mattered. Nothing else had ever been so important. She tried to yell his name, but it came out as a harsh whisper to no one's ears but her own.

Time passed in a sudden flash. She found herself in a heap at Max's doorstep, hitting the bottom part of door in front of her with her palm and looking over her shoulder for the first time. She didn't see her pursuer. The door swung open, causing her upper body, which was leaning into it, to spill forward into the cabin. Max appeared in front of her, and his presence brought forth the sobs hovering just below her throat.

"Charlie!" he exclaimed. He bent and grasped her arms, hauling her the rest of the way inside.

Max looked around outside briefly before he closed the door and locked it.

"Oh, Max," she cried when he swept her into his arms off the floor.

"What happened?" He carried her to the sofa and set her down. His brow creased into a million worried lines as he examined her. "Why aren't you wearing shoes? You're bleeding!"

"I-I had to run. I didn't have time... He was trying to..." Charlotte couldn't spit out a sentence. She still gasped for air.

"Never mind. Hush. Don't try to speak until you've calmed down. My God, you're trembling all over. Take a deep breath, honey, and let it out slowly. You're going to be just fine."

Charlotte sucked in a shaky breath and let it out slowly as instructed.

"Good girl. Breathe like that again and keep on doing it."

Charlotte focused on her breathing as Max cleaned the cuts on the bottom of her feet with a wet rag. Jim walked out from his bedroom and stared at her with a look of horror. "Miss Rose, are you all right?"

Charlotte nodded. She sobbed with relief as the terror receded. She had made it to Max. She would live.

"Find her a handkerchief, Jim. And a quilt too."

Max finished cleaning her bruised and bloodied feet and set the rag aside. Charlotte blew her nose using the handkerchief Jim provided while Max placed the quilt on the sofa. He lifted Charlotte into it and folded it around her snugly. Sitting next to her, he wrapped an arm around her shoulders and pulled her to his side. He kissed her forehead and said with a modicum of humor, "Which would you prefer, darlin', tea or whiskey?"

Charlotte could tell Max was trying to help her feel better by lightening the mood, though his voice still sounded worried. "Tea," she said softly.

"Aren't you a good girl?" He gave her an affectionate squeeze and another kiss. He glanced at Jim, who was standing by the sofa with the same scared expression he'd been wearing since first seeing her. "Jim, would you mind brewing some tea for Charlotte? But bring whiskey for me, and for yourself too if you like. Looks like you could use some."

Jim nodded and walked to the kitchen. Charlotte's tears stopped falling and her heartbeat slowed as Max stroked her arms and back and brushed the hair away from her wet face.

"So, sweetheart, who do I need to kill for causing you such distress?"

Charlotte wiped the tears on her cheek with the backs of her hands. She met his eyes. "Me."

Max lifted an eyebrow. "You? Well, I don't know that I want to kill you just yet, but it sounds like someone's going to get a smacked bottom after a good night's sleep. No one scares my girl like this without getting punished, not even you." He smiled at her.

Charlotte returned a wan smile before sobering with the realization that she'd have to tell him what led her to his doorstep. She gazed into his eyes dolefully. "Max, tomorrow I was going to tell you why I'm no longer living at the boardinghouse, but then I was forced to run here before I could."

He frowned. "What do you mean? I don't understand. Where are you living, if not at the boardinghouse?"

"Nowhere as of today, but I planned to sleep at the schoolhouse tonight."

Max continued to frown at her, looking very

perplexed and worried.

She sighed and said wearily, "Can I tell you what happened tomorrow? I don't feel I have the strength to tell you tonight."

The muscles in Max's face relaxed a bit. "Of course, honey. I think that's a good idea. We'll talk tomorrow."

Jim returned and handed Charlotte her tea and Max a shot of whiskey. Max drank it, then said, "After your tea, Charlotte, you're going to bed. I'll sleep here on the sofa."

Charlotte nodded. She thanked Jim for the tea and took a sip. It felt like warm comfort gliding down her throat and heating her stomach, and it helped to settle her nerves. Charlotte basked in the comfort of Max's embrace and blushed when she became aware for the first time that he wasn't wearing a shirt. She studied his chest. It was lighter in hue than his forearms and face, and curly brown hair wisped thinly around his nipples. She found herself wanting to touch him and stroke the hair on his chest down to his flat stomach. Her eyes traveled south to his trousers and she studied the area that covered his manhood. She'd never seen a man's member, and she found herself feeling very curious about what his looked like beneath the fabric. Her eyes traveled back up his chest and then to his face, where she found his eyes fixed on her and an eyebrow raised.

"What in the tarnation are you staring at, Charlie? You're eyeing me like you've never see a man without a shirt before."

Charlotte blushed harder. "I don't know that I have."

"Well, it's nothing impressive, and I think you've had a good enough gawk for now. Let's get you into bed, why don't we?"

"All right, Max." Charlotte took a final sip and set her teacup on the table next to the sofa. She winced upon standing on her bruised feet.

Max noticed and grabbed her into his arms. He strode to his bedroom. "Blasted woman. What am I going to do with you? You can't even walk."

She let out a moan. "And tomorrow I won't be able to sit," she said mournfully.

"Damn straight." Max placed her on the bed gently. He bent and planted a chaste kiss on her lips, which sent her stomach aflutter. "Rest up, darlin'. You're safe, and everything else will be made right as rain tomorrow."

He straightened and turned to leave, but Charlotte grasped his hand. "Max, will you sleep here with me tonight? I know it's improper, but I don't want you to stop holding me. It comforts me, and I still feel frightened."

Max stared at her for a moment with a conflicted expression, then climbed into bed behind her. He pulled her into his arms. "I don't know how on earth I could say no to that, sweetheart." He kissed the shell of her ear and then her neck, which sent a shiver of delight down her spine. Charlotte snuggled her back into his chest. She shoved her bottom into his crotch and squirmed to get comfortable, not realizing her doing so would elicit a growl from the man holding her.

"None of that, Charlie, unless you want that smacked bottom tonight." He added some space between their lower bodies.

"Maybe I do," she said with a giggle, believing in that moment that any way Max placed his hands on her body would suit her just fine.

"Go to sleep," he ordered in a serious voice.

Charlotte sighed, feeling both comfortable and unsatisfied. She fell asleep in Max's arms, and the morning came much too soon. She awoke to an empty bed and the sounds of Max and Jim talking in the other room. After limping across the room, she looked in the small mirror over the dresser and smoothed her hair down as best she could. She did the same for her dress. Using the pitcher and basin on the dresser, she washed her face and drank some water before exiting the bedroom and meeting Max and Jim in the kitchen.

The mood in the room was tense, and Max and Jim ceased speaking upon her arrival. Neither was sitting at the table but instead standing next to the counter. Bacon sizzled in a pan, and the smell of it along with eggs and toast filled her nose, making her realize how hungry she was. She hadn't eaten since the previous morning. Max looked somber when he regarded her. "Come have some breakfast, Charlotte," he said, his voice stern.

She walked to the table gingerly and sat down. Max fixed her a plate of food in silence, then set it in front of her. Charlotte whispered her thanks and took a bite of the scrambled eggs.

Jim appeared subdued and had a guilty expression on his face. "Feeling all right, Miss Rose?" he asked.

"Much better this morning. Thanks, Jim." She bit into a piece of bacon.

"How are your feet?" Max asked.

"Not bad. I can walk without pain if I don't step too hard."

Max nodded once to indicate that the news was to his liking.

Jim cleared his throat. "I'll be going to the shop now." His shoulders slumped as he walked to the door. He retrieved his Stetson from the hat rack and looked back at Max, who was observing his exit with a frown. "I'm sorry, Max, for not telling you sooner. I wanted to be the one to solve my own problems."

Max was sharp in his response. "Your problems are my problems. I'm very disappointed you think otherwise. We'll discuss it more later."

Jim nodded sadly. He walked out and closed the door. Max remained in the same place for a moment staring at the door before he sat at the table with a mug of freshly brewed coffee.

Max's ill temper made Charlotte nervous. "I gather he told you about the scholarship situation?" She bit into her toast, not tasting a thing.

"Yes, and I'm not pleased with him, or with you, young lady, for knowing about it and not telling me. I don't appreciate secrets being kept from me, especially when they involve the safety of people I care about. Jim seems to think Simon might've had something to do with whatever happened to you last night, which is why he chose to tell me now. Is that the case?"

Charlotte kept her eyes on her plate. "I'm afraid so, and I'm afraid you'll be even more displeased with me upon learning what happened. I'm worried about telling you, Max."

Max took a drink of his coffee. She felt his stern gaze on her face. "Sounds as though you should be worried, Charlotte, but you'd better come clean. I expect to hear the entire truth, and I'm warning you, it would be unwise to do otherwise."

She nodded, then ate another piece of bacon slowly, gathering up her courage while she chewed. Finally she swallowed and explained what brought her to his doorstep.

* * *

Charlotte sat at her desk in the schoolhouse late on Friday afternoon, her carpetbag of belongings beside her. She racked her brain to come up with a solution to what had just happened. She'd miscounted, and the rent had been due to the landlady that day, three days before her second paycheck was due to arrive. Since she'd given all of her first paycheck to Max, she couldn't pay it. No amount of bargaining or explaining would move the woman to wait for the money. The landlady informed her that she had a waiting list of people who wanted to rent a room in her establishment, and she'd only selected the schoolmarm as a boarder under the assumption that someone with her education would be responsible.

A tear slid down Charlotte's face as she remembered the rebuke and the slam of the door behind her as she was evicted. She'd looked back once to find Simon Evans peering at her through his window on the second floor, a smirk on his face, which he couldn't remove in time for her not to see. She wondered how soon the news would travel around town, eventually reaching Max's ears. She felt a knot in her stomach at the thought. It would be better if he heard it from her. She knew this, but she didn't know if she could bring herself to tell him right away.

She buried her head in her arms on the desk until a noise at the door startled her out of her sad thoughts. She lifted her head and took in a sharp breath when Simon Evans strode through. He headed straight for her. She immediately felt like she was in danger, and she searched her mind for a reason to steady her beating heart and settle her panic. It was broad daylight in the middle of town. Surely the man wouldn't risk being caught in the act of harming her.

"I thought I'd find you here," he said.

She stood. "Hello, Mr. Evans. I noticed that you witnessed my eviction from the boardinghouse."

He stopped in front of her desk and ran his long, bony fingers along the smooth wood. Laughing, he said, "Yes, I couldn't help but notice. I imagine many people did. Have you told your beau yet?"

She hesitated, then lied. "Yes, he is meeting me here. In fact he should be here any minute."

"That's interesting," he responded cheerfully. "I just saw him and he mentioned he was headed to the jailhouse to deliver some shackles to the marshal."

"Well, yes," she stammered. "He's coming here after that, of course."

Simon laughed again. "Of course. Well, my dear. I only stopped by to give you some information that might be helpful. There's a room for rent just outside of town. The fee is lower, if that's what your problem is."

"Thank you," Charlotte said, feeling her heartbeat slow to a regular level. "Where is it?"

"Just head west along the main path. It's about a mile out. Nice little green cottage. White picket fence. You can't miss it." He turned to leave. Before he reached the door he looked back. "Good day, Miss Rose. I wish you better luck at your next dwelling." With that, he walked out, closing the door softly behind him.

Charlotte considered his words about the cottage. She found the man repugnant, but she couldn't think of any reason for why he might lie about the available room. Perhaps he was making an effort to be neighborly. She resolved to stay three nights in the schoolhouse, then use the money she received on Monday to rent a room at the cottage, if a room was truly available.

She also decided to tell Max about her eviction, but not until the following day. She needed to work out how to tell him. She felt embarrassed and ashamed, and she knew Max would view her as even more foolish than he already thought her to be.

Evening fell. She removed her shoes and stockings and arranged her carpetbag on the floor to use as a pillow. She kept her dress on and draped the clothes she wasn't wearing over her body in the absence of blankets. It was a warm evening, which was lucky, because she wouldn't have wanted to light the fire in the wood-burning stove and call attention to the fact that someone was inside during odd hours.

Alone on the hard floor, Charlotte felt depressed and near tears. She wallowed in her misery and reconsidered the wisdom in her decision to live on her own in a strange place. She hadn't even been in town for two months and she'd already made a large, irreversible error. Her eviction would undoubtedly become known to the parents of the children, and they would think less of her. Perhaps even the children would cease to respect her.

As she drifted into what promised to be a fitful sleep, she heard a rattling noise at the door. She started fully awake and bolted to a seated position. The schoolhouse door had a lock, but it was a flimsy one, and there was no deadbolt. Her heartbeat quickened as she listened to what sounded like metal scraping metal. Someone was attempting to pick the lock.

"Who's there?" she shouted, her voice shaky but insistent. The scraping noise stopped. "Who's at the door?" she yelled again, a little louder.

When no one responded and the sound resumed, a wave of terror washed over her. Someone was trying to get inside, even knowing she was there. Her gaze darted around the room as she thought about a reason for why that might be. She realized it was likely *because* she was there. Only one person knew of her whereabouts, and it was the one person she knew to be dangerous. The awful thought of Simon visiting her alone in the dark unbidden spurred her into action.

She scrambled to her feet and stumbled to the window, where she struggled to open it. When it stuck even against the entire weight of her body, she let out a panicked whimper and redoubled her efforts. She stepped a few paces away and ran at it, throwing her shoulder into the heavy glass when she reached it. It budged, but only a crack. When she tried to push it again, it didn't move. She stopped and stared at the window's small opening, her mind racing to find a solution. A thought came to her. She ran to the stove and grabbed the poker. She shoved the sharp end of it into the small crack and used it to pry open more space. It worked. After several hard tugs, the crack became wider. With both hands she pushed out, eventually opening the window enough to slip through it. She fled the moment her bare feet touched the ground.

CHAPTER EIGHT

Max didn't speak for some time after hearing the story. He stared at her, and Charlotte watched myriad emotions cross his face—anger, relief, and consternation among them.

When he finally spoke, it was in a low voice that held a slight tremor. "I'm going to kill that man. He is evil, through and through. If nothing else, he needs to be arrested and locked up."

Charlotte sighed. "The problem is, I don't know for sure it was Simon. I never saw him, so I don't think the marshal will arrest him."

Max ran a hand along the stubble on his jaw. "No, I reckon not."

"I'm sorry, Max. Are you terribly angry with me?"

"Right now I feel more relief than anger, Charlotte. That story could have ended much worse. I'm glad you had the wits to escape. That was smart thinking, using a poker to pry open the window." He stood and walked to the counter to pour more coffee into his mug, then took a seat back at the table. "I also feel disheartened that the two people I care about most keep secrets from me. You should have told me no funds were available from Dallas instead of lying to me about it. Then you had another chance to tell me before things went south. I could have helped you keep your room at the boardinghouse. Am I that unapproachable?"

Charlotte shook her head mournfully. "It's not like that, Max. You're so, I don't know, noble and sacrificing. It's the same reason Jim didn't tell you immediately of his troubles. He didn't want you to suffer on his behalf, and I wanted you to be paid for your hard work. I knew you would refuse if I told you the circumstances."

Her response caused Max's eyes to flash with sudden fury. "Your stubborn pride didn't have anything to do with it, then. Is that what you're saying, Charlotte? Because it seems to me that you'd rather be homeless than admit a mistake to me. And it seems that Jim was so hell-bent on proving he's a man that he didn't wish to ask for my assistance when he needed it most."

Charlotte wrung her hands and stared at them. "That's part of it. I will admit that pride did have something to do with my lack of forthrightness. I didn't want to prove you right."

"What in the Sam Hill do you mean, prove me right?"

Charlotte felt tears coming to her eyes. She hated being scolded, and she hated having to admit that his opinion of her mattered, perhaps more than it should. "I know you think me foolish. I allowed myself to get ill with heatstroke. I almost burned my hand on a hot iron. I asked for your labor before verifying I had the money to pay for it. I couldn't even do my figuring right or count out the days of the month correctly."

Charlotte felt her lower lip tremble, and she struggled to say the rest without crying. "It seems I've made nothing but mistakes since I got here. You think I'm a silly girl who needs to be told what to do because I'm weak and foolish. I don't want you to see me that way. I want you to respect me like I respect you."

Max stared at her in disbelief. When he responded, his voice was firm. "I don't think you're foolish or weak, Charlotte, and I respect you a great deal. I think you're young and have some learning to do, but I also think you're gritty and will do just fine. I want to help you along the path I know you'll follow anyway, but you allowed me to become a stumbling block. That gets my dander up. I would have gladly done that work for nothing but a smile from you."

Charlotte stared at him with similar disbelief. "But you said I was a foolish woman the day you met me."

Max rubbed his forehead. "You were acting foolishly, and I was riled up because your illness scared me. That doesn't mean I think you're a foolish person overall."

"I, I'm sorry, Max," she stammered. "Thank you for saying you believe in me. It means a lot, hearing you say that."

Max sighed and leaned back in his chair. "And I certainly don't think you're weak. I can't believe you don't know how brave I think you are. Why, even after passing out from heatstroke, you dusted yourself off in two shakes and proceeded to tell me off again like nothing had happened. If that ain't a woman with more than one round of lead in her gun, I don't know what is."

Charlotte gave him a small smile, and he smiled back at her before becoming serious again. "I want you to promise me something, Charlotte."

"Yes, Max?"

"Promise me that you'll admit future mistakes to me. In return, I promise to treat you kindly when you do. I want only to support you, and I don't want your stubborn pride in the way of me being able to do so."

Charlotte swallowed and nodded. "I promise. Thank you."

"Do you recall what you said when I spanked you? I sure do. You said you felt vulnerable but not scared. That's a good thing. That's how a woman should feel with her man. I want you to feel that way without a spanking. I want you to come to me with your foolish mistakes, knowing that even if I discipline you, it will be with love, without mockery, and with the intention of making things better."

She nodded her agreement. "I want that too."

"How did it make you feel, keeping those big secrets from me?"

A tear slid down her face. "I felt lonely and scared."

"Right. If you'd told me, you wouldn't have felt either. You would've had my full support and protection. Instead, your stubborn pride caused you to lie and carry the burden yourself. Worse, it allowed you to compromise your safety. What do you think I should do about that, as the man responsible for your safety?"

Charlotte looked down and stirred the eggs on her plate, her cheeks growing warm. She understood that he expected her to say he should punish her, and she felt embarrassed. She thought she would be spanked, but she didn't think she'd have to be amenable to it. This was part of it, she realized. Max was forcing her to let go of some of her pride even before punishment.

"I suppose you should punish me," she said with a giant sigh.

"I think I should too." Max stood. He cupped Charlotte's chin with his hand and tilted it up. He had a determined, set look on his face that was very stern. She recognized that expression. It was the same look he wore when he ordered her over his lap the last time. It made her feel calm, in a way.

His resolve allowed her to obey without feeling the need to argue, since she knew it would be useless to do so anyway.

"This will be a real punishment, Charlotte, not a few smacks. I told you I wouldn't be lenient if I had to spank you again for safety reasons, and I don't intend to be. Finish your breakfast, then join me on the sofa."

"Yes, sir," she said as she felt a nervous flop in her tummy.

She bit into her toast as he strode to the living room. She didn't feel the least bit hungry anymore, but she ate anyway. She knew she would do well to finish a meal, and she also wanted to delay the punishment. When the food was gone from her plate, she slowly washed the dish in the basin until she heard Max's voice call out to her.

"That can wait. Come here, Charlotte."

She sighed and walked to where Max sat in the middle of the sofa. When she reached him, he said simply, "Skirts up and over my lap."

Charlotte did as instructed. Her face flamed as she positioned herself over his legs. Regardless of whether she felt she deserved it, it was terribly embarrassing. Max hugged her body to his and rubbed her bottom a couple times, like he was getting a feel for his target. The thinness of the drawers felt obvious then, since they did little to diminish the way his touch felt on her body.

Without further delay, Max inflicted two hard swats, one on each cheek, and she yelped.

The following swats were moderate and without pause, much different from how her original spanking had felt. At first she thought it wouldn't be too bad, since his hand wasn't striking as hard as it had the first time. However, Charlotte felt the sting growing after a minute, and she whimpered.

"How long are you going to spank me, Max?" she asked, feeling more worried with every swat that followed the previous without slowing.

"Until I believe you've learned your lesson, young lady." His swats fell harder and more briskly after her question, making it apparent he didn't appreciate her asking. Charlotte squirmed.

"What lesson are you learning right now?" he asked.

Charlotte winced, and her mind raced to find the right answer in the midst of her discomfort. "That I'm not to keep secrets from you."

"That's right, at least not any that could affect your safety. What else?" Max lowered his punishing hand and connected it with her thighs, which were also only thinly covered by her drawers.

She yelped at a particularly hard smack and suddenly felt angry. She hadn't known it would hurt so much, or she never would have said she deserved it. "Stop, Max! I insist that you stop this right now."

Max stopped abruptly, and she breathed a sigh of relief. Her relief was quickly replaced by dismay when she felt the ribbon of her drawers loosen and a breeze of cool air brush her bare bottom and thighs as he slid the material to her ankles. She froze as he bared her. The confusion over how she felt rendered her speechless. She had never been exposed in such a way to a man, and she felt both aroused and embarrassed. Tears welled up in her eyes as his hand cracked down with renewed vigor. A short time later, she shrieked at the intensity of the heat his hand was igniting on her bared skin and frantically reached back to protect her tender seat, while doing everything in her power to remain still over his thighs. She didn't want to move in such a way that would reveal to his eyes the aroused area between her legs.

Max caught her wrist and anchored it against her waist without slowing the swats. "You don't get to decide when your spanking ends, Charlotte, and you also don't get to speak to me in angry, demanding tones during discipline. Now is the time to be contrite and accepting of your well-deserved punishment. Any other attitude will make it worse for you."

She felt angrier with every swat. "I can't believe you would force me to endure a spanking without my drawers. It's humiliating, and it hurts terribly." She said the last words in a self-pitying whimper.

Max paused again and ran his hand over her bottom to her thigh, where it settled lightly. How his hand felt so gentle one moment and so hard the next kept Charlotte bewildered and on high alert. She was aware of his every touch and movement, and every time he spoke, the deep timbre of his voice made her heart pound.

"You know what would've been worse than this spanking, Charlotte? If Simon had caught you. You've behaved badly and put yourself in danger. You've been stubborn, prideful, and disobedient. I'm punishing you sternly to teach you a lesson in the hopes that I won't have to repeat it. So, I'll ask you again. What else are you learning from this?"

Her nether region constricted and she clamped her thighs together. It was all so overwhelming to her—the pain, the arousal, the embarrassment. She growled in frustration. "I'm learning that you're a brute, Maxwell Harrison!"

His hand moved up from her thigh and patted her bottom. "Wrong answer, darlin'."

She moaned and grasped the cushion of the sofa with her free hand, suspecting that he would make her pay for that remark. She was right. He resumed the swats to the sound of her corresponding yelps of protest. Her tears fell freely and soon she was sobbing and kicking, no longer concerned with modesty. Her crying didn't move Max and he continued on, peppering every inch of her bottom and upper thighs with stinging swats.

His unrelenting punishment finally pushed her to the state of mind she'd felt before, the place where her pride and outrage turned to vulnerability and the need to be comforted. "M-Max," she sobbed. "I'm sorry I was too proud to admit my mistake to you. I will do better in the future."

Those were the right words said in the right tone. Max's hand finally settled. "All right then, sweetheart." He rubbed her back and murmured, "Stubborn, stubborn girl. Yeah?"

Charlotte sniffled and nodded.

"If ever there was a woman who needed a good spanking every once in a while, it would be you, honey." He rubbed her burning backside, soothing it with his touch while his words soothed her feelings.

Charlotte couldn't bring herself to agree with him, so she apologized instead. "I'm sorry I said you were a brute."

"You're forgiven. I reckon it's nicer than thief or ruffian, in any case."

"Will you hold me?" she asked in a small voice.

"Of course. Come here, honey." He gathered her right side up on his lap and held her close. He kissed her forehead, both wet cheeks, and her pouting lips. "That just about wrecked me, you asking that. I will always hold you, for as long as you need, whenever you need it."

Sitting on Max's lap with a sore bottom gave her a feeling of contentedness like nothing else. She marveled over how loved she felt in that moment. It felt so much better than holding onto her pride and suffering her mistakes alone. Max punished her, but he also supported and loved her.

Max confirmed the way he felt when his lips brushed her ear with a kiss and he whispered, "I hope you know I love you, Charlotte Rose."

Charlotte gave him a watery-eyed smile and wrapped her arms around his neck. She knew without a doubt that he did, and she returned the sentiment.

CHAPTER NINE

Max and Charlotte walked hand in hand to the shop. Max had offered to hook up his horse and buggy for the journey to town because of Charlotte's scraped feet, but she walked a few paces in his cabin and determined she would be fine. Upon arriving at the shop, they found Jim shaping metal hangers for the seamstress. He looked forlorn sitting alone in the corner of the room.

Max walked to Jim and tousled his hair. "Let's the three of us have a chinwag, scamp. We're going to work out this nasty business."

Jim's eyes took on a glimmer of hope upon hearing Max's lighthearted tone. He set his work down and brushed aside the light hair draping his eyes.

Max positioned chairs next to where Jim sat on his bench, and he and Charlotte each took a seat. "Three things I want to say to you, Jim, before we get to the less pleasant conversation about Simon. One is, I understand why you didn't want to tell me about your troubles, but you must understand that something like this shouldn't be kept secret from me."

Jim nodded slowly. "I understand that now, Max."

"Good. Second, I didn't express before how proud I am that you were offered a scholarship. The way I see it, you're as rare as a blue horse. I reckon you're the only lad I know who's good at book-learning *and* working with his hands."

Jim's face lit up. He beamed at Max and looked at Charlotte, who was smiling as well.

"Third," Max continued in a mock serious tone. "You need a haircut."

Jim brushed away more hair from his face and smiled. "Yeah, I reckon I do."

Max winked and then cleared his throat. "All right, now that the important stuff is out of the way, we need to discuss what to do about Simon."

Charlotte explained to Jim her suspicion that Simon tried to break into the schoolhouse and then pursued her with ill intent.

Jim's eyes widened and he addressed Max after hearing her story. "This is what I was afraid of. Simon will take it out on other people if I don't do his bidding. I should go away and let him have the money."

Max shook his head. "That's out of the question. By doing so, you'd be playing part in a crime. You could go to jail for something like that, especially if Simon manages to pin the theft on you."

Jim responded with frustration. "So I should go against Simon and stay, even if my staying is a danger to you and Miss Rose? You don't know my father like I do, Max. He doesn't suffer losing without making others suffer worse."

"He's only one man, Jim. One man doesn't get to have control over three people's lives. Now I know we don't have proof of his plan, but I say we report this to the marshal. He might know what to do about it."

Jim took in a sharp breath. "He'll kill me, Max. I know he'll kill me or you if he finds out we took this to the law. He as good as said that to me already."

Charlotte reached out and touched his hand. "No, Jim. Max is right. We need to tell the marshal. If Simon comes for you, Max or the marshal will protect you."

"I can protect myself," he said sullenly.

Charlotte removed her hand, sorry she had offended the boy.

Max said, "We're all going to protect each other." He rubbed the back of his neck. "I have an important question for you, Jim. And I want you to think about it and not answer right away. All right?"

That got Jim's attention. His eyes snapped back to Max's face. "Sure."

"Would you be interested in going to college

on that scholarship, if there was a way to get Simon out of the picture?"

Jim looked surprised. "I don't know. I just assumed you wouldn't want me to go, so I haven't really thought on it."

"That's not the case, Jim. I want whatever you want. That scholarship is kind of a big deal. It might be foolish to pass it up. Am I right, Charlie?"

She nodded. "Colleges don't give out scholarships to people unless they have real talent, Jim."

Max added, "You could always come back and work with me after college if you really wanted to. It wouldn't be goodbye either way."

Jim scratched his head. "I dunno. I guess I need to think about it more before giving you an answer."

Max nodded once. "Good lad. In the meantime, let's go have a chat with the marshal."

* * *

Marshal Huntley listened with a neutral expression and without interrupting while Jim described the planned theft. The marshal sat behind his wooden desk, and the three of them sat across from him. When Jim finished speaking, the marshal leaned forward, rested his elbows on the desk, and folded his hands in front of him.

"I'll tell you what I can and can't do," he said,

focusing his attention on Jim. "I'm sorry to say I can't arrest him, since we don't have evidence. What I can do is send an official telegram as well as a more detailed letter of explanation to the college to let them know of your knowledge of the planned theft."

"That's a good idea," Max said. "Surely a college wouldn't give the man money after hearing about his character from a lawman. That should just about solve the problem when it comes to misuse of funds, don't you think?"

"Just about. If Jim wants to go to college, I'll suggest they transfer the funds to you, Max." The marshal leaned back in his chair and scowled. "I'm more concerned about the threats of violence Simon has made. I plan to speak with him about that and use some threats of my own."

Charlotte spoke for the first time since saying hello when she entered the jailhouse. "Marshal, I suspect he tried to harm me already."

The marshal's expression was not as neutral as she related what happened at the schoolhouse after being evicted. His scowl became more pronounced the longer she spoke. Max's jaw clenched as he listened to the story being told for the third time.

"That's more than a little disturbing," the marshal said. "Where do you plan to stay now, Miss Rose? You can't stay at the schoolhouse."

"She'll stay with me," Max asserted with finality.

Charlotte looked over at him. "That wouldn't be proper, Max. What would people think, me staying at your place without us being married?"

Max waved his hand in her direction dismissively. "I'll marry you then, Charlie."

Charlotte scowled. "Maxwell Harrison," she said, rising to her feet. "That was the worst marriage proposal in the history of proposals."

Max got a sheepish look on his face. The marshal laughed and continued laughing for some time. "I'm sorry," he said, still laughing.

"Why's that so funny, marshal?" Charlotte asked, staring at him.

The marshal eventually sobered enough to speak. "Ah, well. Let's just say my wife might disagree about that being the worst proposal, Miss Rose. She didn't exactly get the bent-knee proposal she might have wanted. My knee was bent all right, but she was over it when I asked."

Jim and Max snickered, and Charlotte's face turned a shade of pink. "I suppose I shouldn't complain then," she said wryly, and sat back down. "What is it with you men out here? Is there a woman in Texas without a sore backside?"

The marshal laughed again, and Max reached for her hand. "What do you say, darlin'? Fancy me for a husband?"

Charlotte huffed and frowned at him, but her frown transformed into a smile as she looked into his twinkling eyes. "I admit the prospect of marrying you is not entirely displeasing to me."

Max laughed and kissed her hand. "If mine was the worst proposal, then that was the worst answer to one."

The marshal grinned. "Bet you're glad I didn't ask you to join the posse, eh, Max? I think the errand of fetching Miss Rose worked well in your favor."

"Yes," Max agreed. "I reckon it's the greatest thing I ever fetched." He squeezed Charlotte's hand before releasing it. "I'll remind you that I do know how to shoot a gun, though, marshal. I'll be wearing one these days, now that I know what kind of threat we're facing with Simon."

"It's not a bad idea," the marshal admitted, standing. "I hope to ensure it doesn't come to that, though." He crossed the room, removed his gun belt from where it hung, and buckled it around his hips. "I'll start by having a conversation with Simon Evans. Hopefully that's all it'll take."

❈ ❈ ❈

The wedding ceremony was short and sweet, just like their courtship. Charlotte wore her pink taffeta dress, the same dress she wore when she first met Max, which brought a grin to his face.

That night, he laid his wife on the bed and said, "Now I get to take off this pretty gown and spend some time looking at what's underneath."

She sighed as he slowly unbuttoned the front of her dress. Before he removed it entirely, he glided a hand under her shift to touch her breasts. Charlotte's breath hitched as he massaged and flicked a nipple with his thumb.

"More than a handful, just like you," he murmured, and bent to enclose her lips in a kiss. He couldn't get enough of her, and his kisses became deeper and more sensual as his hands roamed her body. Her tongue played with his until he released her from his kiss long enough to peel the layers of clothes off her body. When her naked form stretched out in all of its raw beauty on the bed, he continued his ministrations. She let out a soft moan when he kissed her lightly along the collarbone. Her hands fumbled with the buttons of his shirt. He smiled and collected her wrists in his left hand, then placed them high above her head on the bed.

Charlotte looked at him in a haze of desire. "I want to touch you. Please," she begged.

He kissed her again while still holding her wrists above her head, then peppered her with kisses along her chin to her neck. "Where would you like to touch me, my love?" he asked huskily against her neck. "Here?" He laid his right hand on her breast.

"Mm hmm." She nodded and arched into his touch.

"How about here?" he asked, raking his fingertips down her soft torso.

She mewled her answer. "Yes, Max."

"And here too?" He released her hands and wrapped both of his around her delicate waist.

"I want to touch you everywhere," she said eagerly.

"Mmm," he intoned. "That sounds nice, darlin'." Max moved his hand to between her legs. Her eyes met his and widened as he teased his fingers along her wet slit and circled her nub of nerves. Pinching and flicking, he took her nearly to the height of pleasure before he removed his hand, causing her to whimper. He worked out the buttons on his shirt and shrugged the material off, while she watched his every movement. Unbuttoning his trousers, he watched her gaze travel south to his erection, which he exposed when he shucked off the pants.

Her eyes rounded and she stared at him unabashedly. He chuckled, took her hand, and pulled her into a seated position. She sat on the edge of the bed and held her palms against his chest. As her hands moved down his front, she asked, "Does it feel as good when I touch you as it does when you touch me?"

"Yes, darlin', I'd wager so." Max's head tilted back when both of her small, soft hands wrapped around his cock. A few moments later, his eyes snapped back to her face. She grinned at him.

"What are you doing?"

"Playing," she said, and rubbed the side of his rock-hard cock against her cheek. "It's strange.

It feels really hard but the skin is so soft."

He groaned and allowed her to play with him until he couldn't take it any longer, which was the moment she slapped his cock against her cheek. He gathered her arms, lifted her, and positioned her on her back on the bed. "My turn to play," he grunted. His body slid over hers, grazing her breasts and belly. With his knee, he guided her legs apart and then pressed the head of his cock against her entrance. He listened to her small gasps as he slid into her tight warmth slowly until he reached the barrier inside of her, where he paused.

"You feel so good," he groaned. "My god."

She wrapped her legs around him, drawing him into her. With one slow, strong thrust he ruptured her hymen and caught the cry coming from her lips with his kiss. Every nerve in his body demanded that he pound into her again, harder, but he waited until her cry faded into a whimper before he began his movements, He forced himself to be gentle and slow. "I know it hurts the first time, my love. Are you all right?" he murmured in her ear.

"Yes," she said and wrapped her arms around his neck. "I love how it feels now. It's so strong, the feeling I have."

"Good girl. Let that feeling build."

She came soon after, which surprised and relieved Max, as he didn't think he would've been able to hold off for very long with her virgin canal so tightly clenched around him. As soon as she wailed and arched her back, his release followed, and he spilled his seed inside of her. With one final thrust, he pulled out and collapsed next to her on his back, breathing hard.

Charlotte rolled over to him and rested her head in the crook of his arm and shoulder. She traced circles on his chest, and he cuddled her into him and kissed her forehead. While entangled in each other's embrace, they talked about how they envisioned their future together, how many children they wanted, how Jim would be like a big brother to them, and other happy topics that they smiled and sighed about. In that moment, life seemed just about perfect.

* * *

Jim decided to use the scholarship and attend college after again receiving Max's assurance that he could return to work for him as a blacksmith if he so desired. Although Max was proud of Jim and thought he made the right choice, he mourned it and expressed his sadness to Charlotte. He knew it was unlikely that Jim would return to blacksmithing. The only hope Max allowed himself to feel was that Jim would return to Texas eventually and take another occupation that suited his education. He didn't like the thought of Jim being gone for good.

Because of the marshal's official report to the college regarding Simon's planned theft, the dean altered the scholarship's disbursement plan in a couple of ways. He elected to only send Max enough money to pay for Jim's travel expenses and room and board during his journey east. The rest of the scholarship money would be paid directly to the professors at the college and the landlord at the dormitory where Jim would reside.

Simon made himself so scarce after the marshal visited him that Max was tempted to dismiss him as a threat. He resisted doing so, however, knowing that letting his guard down could have dire consequences. He wore his Remington at all times except while sleeping, when he kept it next to the bed. He escorted Charlotte to and from the schoolhouse so that she was never alone, and he kept Jim close as well. Jim discontinued attending his book club and instead walked home with Max and Charlotte after each work day.

A month before Jim was to depart, the money for his travels was wired to Max. As much as Max hated the thought of saying goodbye to Jim, he also looked forward to the day. Leaving would finally provide the boy with total freedom from his father, whose very presence in the small town served as a painful reminder of the violence in his past.

CHAPTER TEN

Charlotte grew impatient with the need to be escorted everywhere she went. Although she enjoyed Max's presence most of the time, and found the morning walks to work with him and Jim pleasant, not being allowed to travel home without Max became a serious inconvenience. She would often have to wait for him to finish his work at the shop long after she finished teaching at the schoolhouse. The sounds of banging metal and the heat from the forge gave her a headache, and she wasn't able to do much but sit idly in the shop until Max and Jim finished working.

She complained about it one evening and suggested that in the future Max allow her and Jim to walk home together after she finished teaching. Max was adamant in his refusal. "Absolutely not. You think Simon couldn't overpower you both, especially if he carried a gun?"

"But Max, how long must we live like this?"

she despaired. "I feel like if Simon was going to hurt us, he would have done so by now. The marshal's threat must have worked."

Max shook his head and scowled. "We can't know that for sure, Charlotte. We'll discuss it again after Jim goes to college. Until then, you must stay by my side."

Charlotte glowered at him before she turned and stormed out of the house. Shortly after she slammed the door to the cabin and set out for the barn, the door reopened.

"Get back here," Max called to her, with no attempt to disguise his irritation. "You got cotton in your ears? What did I just say?"

She stopped and turned. "I can't even go to the barn alone? You must be joking."

"Do I look like I'm joking? You have three seconds to get back inside, or you'll be sorry."

Charlotte muttered some unflattering words about her husband under her breath, but obeyed. She walked up the steps to the cabin, gave him a dirty look, and shoved past him to the kitchen. "You don't have to speak to me like I'm a child, you know," she flung over her shoulder.

Max closed the front door. "Maybe I do, since you're pitching a fit like a child."

Jim eyed the two of them warily, then excused himself to his room, clearly uncomfortable to be present while they argued. Max sighed and sat in his armchair. He picked up his book on the side table and tried to read while

Charlotte banged around the kitchen. She made as much noise as possible while she rearranged the pots and pans for no reason other than to give her hands something to do and to annoy Max. She transferred the silverware into a different drawer, dropping in each spoon, knife, and fork in it one by one from a height that made the clanging noise louder than necessary.

Max closed his book with a thud. "Are you nearly finished making that ruckus?"

Charlotte responded by slamming a cupboard door.

"I've had enough, Charlotte," he said in a low, even voice.

Charlotte spun to face him. "And I've had enough of your blasted nannying! I can't live like this. I feel like a prisoner." She knew she was acting childish, but she felt angry and unable to contain her fury.

Max set his book on the table beside him and spoke gently. "I know it's not easy, Charlotte, but it won't be like this forever."

His calm demeanor only infuriated her further. "I can't take another day of it!" She grabbed the closest thing in her reach, a plate, and launched it across the room. It shattered into pieces when it hit the wall.

Max looked as shocked as she felt. She could hardly believe what she'd just done, and she gaped at the mess on the floor. Max strode to her, grasped her chin, and forced her to meet his flashing eyes.

"I've endured your ill temper," he said through gritted teeth, "but now you've used up my supply of patience for today. I suggest you calm yourself."

She shook her face out of his hand and turned to walk away, but he took hold of her arms. She tried to shrug him off, but her flailing did nothing to free her. He continued to hold onto her with his unyielding hands. "Settle down, Charlie!"

Her inability to get loose made her feel angrier and more frantic. Since her arms were of no use to hit him, she tried to kick him, but Max anticipated it and stepped to the side. He grunted and spun her around. "Want to provoke me, do you? How do you think that's going to end for you?"

"Don't!" she cried as he held her arm and landed his palm across her bottom. It was a sharp, stinging smack. The force of it stunned her into rational thought. She stilled and braced herself, expecting another. Instead, Max tugged her to their room. Once inside with the door shut, he sat on the bed and toppled her over his lap. Without a word, he yanked up her skirts. She offered no resistance. On some level, she knew she needed to be punished, and she wanted him to take control of the situation. His next words told her he understood exactly what she needed and wanted.

"With that kind of outrageous behavior, Charlie, you might as well be begging me for a spanking. I'd be remiss not to give you one." He pushed her drawers to her ankles, then hauled her forward to lie fully over his left thigh. He draped his other leg over hers, pinning her into place.

Charlotte suspected with dismay that she was about to endure a spanking severe enough to necessitate Max restraining her movements. She was right. She shrieked when his heavy palm first connected with her bare skin and let out a long wail that lasted throughout most of the punishment. From the first swat to the last, Max's hand descended swiftly and without mercy. It was the shortest spanking he'd ever given her—less than a minute—but it was also the hardest, and by the end she sagged over his knee, exhausted and aware of little but the burn she felt on her punished backside and the sensitive area where her bottom met her thighs.

She heard his stern voice through the pain. "Are you finished with your tantrum now, or do you need some more swats?"

She wiped the tears from her cheek. "I'm finished," she whimpered, fully subdued.

He slowly relaxed the leg that pinned her in place and lifted her legs to rest over both of his. He caressed her bottom and thighs. After some time, he asked, "Do you feel better now, darlin'?"

"Yes. Thank you, Max."

She reveled in the comfort she felt from him holding her in such an intimate, vulnerable position. His left hand was anchored around her waist, and his forearm still pinned her to his leg, giving her a sense of security, while his other hand conveyed both warning and solace in its tender strokes over her bottom and legs. She knew he would do whatever it took to keep her safe and in line.

"You're such a good girl, thanking me for your spanking," he murmured, squeezing her burning globes gently before resuming his caress.

"I'm sorry, Max. I know my behavior was appalling. It's just, I feel trapped. I'm used to independence."

Max ran his hand down the length of her body, from shoulder to flank. "If I knew a better way to keep the two of you safe, I'd do it. I know it's hard on you, having to wait for me to finish my work at the shop. But I have a horrible feeling that the moment Simon sees you alone again, like you were that night at the schoolhouse, he'll attack. Nothing scares me more than the thought of you or Jim being harmed. So please, be agreeable to me escorting you, for my sake if not for your own."

Charlotte looked back at him. His worried eyes met hers. She felt her own eyes moisten and a burning in her nose that indicated she was moments from crying again. "I'm sorry. I should have known how much this affected you."

Max gathered her into his arms, and she rested her head against his chest. "All you need to know is how much you mean to me, so you understand why I need to keep you safe."

Charlotte nodded. As she basked in his love, she felt a strong desire to return the favor. She wanted to comfort him or at least distract him from his worry. She moved her body so that she faced him and straddled her legs around his hips. She kissed him deeply while his palms on her back pulled her to him, flattening her breasts against his hard chest.

"Max, I want to make you feel good," she said between kisses.

He opened his eyes and smiled. "You do, Charlie."

"I mean *really* good." She reached down and fumbled with his belt.

He said nothing as she undid the buckle. While unbuttoning his trousers, she shimmied her hips backwards off his lap until her feet reached the floor. She dropped to her knees in front of him.

Max stared at her, his eyes sparking with lust. "Where did you learn about this, young lady?"

Charlotte slid her hand up his cock, which hardened under her touch. Leaning forward, she kissed the head of it tentatively, then looked straight into his eyes as she circled her lips around him and took him into her mouth.

"Oh, sweet Jesus," he moaned.

Through a mouthful of cock, she garbled that the saloon owner's wife had given her advice on how to please a man. Charlotte found a bobbing rhythm and tightened her lips, flicking his cock with her tongue as she did. She peered up at him through her lashes often, thrilled by the bliss she read on his face and the fact that she was the one causing it. Her jaw ached after some time, but she didn't care.

He reached roughly around her head. Lacing his fingers through her hair, his hand tightened into a fist. With a sudden groan, he pulled her head away from him, releasing his cock from her mouth so he could release his warm seed on her face. When he spilled the last of it and relaxed his grip on her hair, she eyed him with surprise. She held her hands under her chin to catch what streamed down her cheek and said, "I thought I was supposed to swallow this."

He snorted out laughter and collapsed backwards on the bed. "Next time, darlin'."

Charlotte stood from her kneeled position and walked to the basin of water, where she washed her hands and face. "What makes you think there will be a next time?" she teased.

He sat up. "Well, for one thing, I saw the look in your eye. You enjoyed that, though not half as much as I did, that's for darn sure."

She looked back at him. "Was I good at it, Max?" she asked sincerely while rubbing her cheek with a wet cloth. It was an honest question. She didn't know whether it was a skill she could rightfully claim to possess.

He laughed loudly and stood. He adjusted himself back into his trousers and buttoned them, then walked to her and gathered her into his arms. "I think my response removed the need to ask that question, darlin', but since you asked... Yes, you were very, very good at it. I'm a lucky man."

Charlotte smiled and returned his hug. "I'm the lucky one. You care enough to protect me."

It was true. Max thought of little else but protecting Charlotte and Jim. His worry over how to continue doing so often kept him up at night, and that night was another in which he couldn't find sleep. He left the bed where Charlotte slept and the gun next to it. He sat on the porch bench and thought about their situation. Until Jim went to college, Max wouldn't feel like Jim was safe, and as long as Simon lived in Porter, Max wouldn't feel like Charlotte was safe. He tried to think of a solution while sipping a glass of whiskey.

Just as he was about to return to bed in an attempt to sleep for a couple of hours before work, something heavy and hard crashed into his skull. In a flash, the world went blacker than the moonless night.

CHAPTER
ELEVEN

The next morning was Sunday, and Charlotte woke up to bright light from the sun streaming into the bedroom. She immediately felt that something was wrong. Ever since she and Max had married, she'd never slept in this late. Max always woke before the crack of dawn even on his day of rest, and his movements stirred her awake every time. She felt an inkling of fear, but she squashed it and determined that he must have been especially quiet in his morning activities that day.

When she didn't find him anywhere else in the cabin, her fear took root. Jim found her standing by the stove with a puzzled expression on her face.

"What's wrong, Charlie?" he asked, noticing her expression. Jim had used that nickname for her since she'd gotten married to Max, and Charlotte had actually grown fond of it.

"I have a terrible feeling, Jim. Max isn't here."

Jim cocked his head. "He's not in your room?"

"No." The fear that had taken root began to grow as she witnessed Jim's facial expression morph into a worried frown that matched her own. They both knew Max wouldn't leave them of his own accord, certainly not without telling them.

Charlotte and Jim walked outside, and Charlotte screamed when she saw the blood on the porch. Jim removed a slip of paper tacked to the door, read it, and handed it to Charlotte. On it was scribbled a simple but devastating threat.

Tell the marshal, and I kill him... slowly.

Charlotte sank to the ground and gasped for air as she hyperventilated and sobbed. Jim had the opposite response to the same strong feeling of horror. He froze and stared, wide-eyed, into the distance. In the moments before he spoke, Jim's expression changed from that of a scared boy into that of a determined man. He reached down and shook one of Charlotte's shoulders.

"We're going to find him. Help me come up with a plan." Jim's stern tone forced Charlotte to her feet. Jim strode inside, found Max's gun and belt next to the bed, and buckled it around his hips.

"Do you know how to shoot that, Jim?" she asked in a trembling voice.

"Better than some. I've pulled a trigger once or twice in my life. Now, where could Simon be keeping him?"

Charlotte shook her head in dismay. "I have no clue!" she cried. "The only place I know Simon to stay is at the boardinghouse, and he wouldn't dare keep Max there."

"No, he wouldn't. He used to own a house outside of town. I thought he sold it, but I don't have any better ideas of where he might be. Do you?"

"No," Charlotte wailed, hardly able to think about how to place one foot in front of the other, let alone how to find her husband.

"Let's go there then."

Jim saddled Max's horse. They rode in the direction of Simon's old house, with Jim in the saddle up front leading the mare and Charlotte riding astride behind him, her skirts hiked to an unladylike distance above her knees, which she didn't notice for a moment.

* * *

Before he opened his eyes, Max felt the heavy twine digging into the skin of his wrists, which were bound behind him around a beam. He sat on dirt ground, and his head pounded with each beat of his heart. His mouth and throat felt dry and gritty with dust. As he drew nearer to consciousness, he drew nearer to dismay. He became aware of the fact that he'd been captured, and that meant he couldn't protect Jim and Charlotte.

He opened his eyes, and the darkness he met in the room was not much brighter than the darkness behind his eyelids. As the seconds ticked by, his eyes slowly adjusted, and the rest of his senses awoke. He was in someone's barn, evident by the smell of hay and manure. The sound of a nickering horse made its way to his ears through the thumping in his head. He struggled against his bonds and quickly learned it would be no use to do so. He was bound too tightly, so much so that the circulation to his fingers was all but cut off entirely. His fingers were numb, and he could barely move them.

The fear in Max grew the longer he sat alone without his kidnapper. Perhaps Simon meant to capture the three of them, and he got Max out of the way first to render the other two helpless to fight him. This thought filled him with such horror that he was relieved when he heard the barn door open and witnessed Simon approaching him, alone. He held a lamp that lit shadows across his face, giving the man an especially evil appearance. Max's throat filled with sudden bile and revulsion at the sight of Simon's pointy, shadowed features.

"It's just you and me now, blacksmith." Simon dragged a wooden stool across the floor and placed it directly in front of Max. He set the lamp on the ground and sat down.

"What the hell do you want, Simon," Max asked, his voice hoarse.

A grin spread across his face. "Revenge," he replied. "If it weren't for you wasting space in this town, things would be different. Jim wouldn't have made such a foolish decision to go against me, and Charlotte wouldn't have been distracted by your strange type of charm, if it can be called that."

"Then kill me and get it over with. But be forewarned that the marshal will know exactly who did it. You'll swing from the highest tree in Porter, and most everyone will come to watch. I regret I won't be in attendance, since I reckon it'll be good entertainment. I can just imagine it, the noose tightening around your lily white neck and your tears dampening the rope before it repays your cowardice with death."

Simon drew back his fist and punched Max so hard that he almost fell unconscious again. His head hung forward, and blood from his nose dripped onto his trousers. Though his voice sounded far away, Max heard Simon say something that sent a chill down his spine.

"I'll be sure to relay your brave words to Jim and Charlotte as I beat them until they beg to die."

❊ ❊ ❊

Jim and Charlotte arrived at the house previously owned by Simon, and Charlotte felt her spirits sink as they neared. At any other time, the sight of children playing in the grass and a mother humming while hanging laundry would have been pleasant, but to Charlotte this meant only one thing—Max wasn't there.

Jim came to the same conclusion at the same time because he said, "We'll keep looking."

He dismounted and spoke to the woman hanging laundry. He asked if he might look in her barn briefly, and the woman granted the small favor. Shortly after peeking inside, Jim walked back to Charlotte and the horse, shaking his head. He remounted.

They rode in the direction of town silently, each knowing that the other was deep in thought about where else Simon might have taken Max. The horse clipped along on the path at a cheerful pace that belied the misery of their journey. As they rode, Charlotte had an idea.

"Jim, I just remembered something. The day I was evicted, Simon informed me of a room for rent in a house. I can't think why he would tell me about it, since it's not in his nature to be helpful."

"You're right about that," Jim replied. "Maybe he owns the house. Where is it, do you know?"

"A mile west of town, according to him. He described it as a green cottage with a white picket fence."

Jim turned the horse around. "I'm trying not to get my hopes up, Charlie, but I think you might've figured out where Simon is keeping Max."

Jim and Charlotte elected to walk the last quarter mile to the house in order to limit the chance of being spotted. The cottage could be seen in the distance. As they neared, it became clear to Charlotte that Simon's description of the place had been exaggerated at best. The green paint peeled away from the wood, and nearly every white fencepost was broken or crooked. Weeds grew tall and thick along the path that led to the door.

A weathered barn stood a few paces away, and the door to it was open. Jim and Charlotte crouched behind a collection of tumbleweeds and observed the house and barn for a long while. Charlotte's legs cramped from the position, but she didn't dare shift lest the noise give away their presence. After what seemed like hours, they saw exactly what they'd hoped to see—Simon exiting the barn and walking to the house. As soon as he closed the door of the house behind him, Jim and Charlotte exchanged a look that they each read perfectly, and they crept at a light jog to the barn together.

Charlotte covered her mouth to stifle a scream when she saw Max's slumped, unconscious body tied to a beam. They rushed to him. Jim pulled out a knife from his pocket. He sliced the twine above Max's purple fingers as Charlotte observed with horror the caked blood in his dark hair.

"Quick," Jim whispered to Charlotte. "We have to get him awake and out of here."

"Max, darling," Charlotte said through her tears. "Wake up." She placed her palm on his hot forehead and trailed her fingers down his bruised cheek. He didn't move.

Jim lightly slapped his face on the side that wasn't bruised and shook his shoulder, to no avail.

"How will we get him out of here? We can't carry him," Charlotte said in a frantic whisper.

"No," Jim agreed. He drew the gun from its holster on his right hip and said, "You keep trying to wake him. I'll stand by the door and watch for Simon."

Jim took his post by the barn's door and Charlotte searched for some clean water. She found a bucket half full of water and sprinkled some on her tongue to test it. Clean enough. She hauled it over to where Max sat and ripped off a strip of her petticoat. After soaking it in the water, she proceeded to dampen Max's face by pressing the cloth against his skin. He moaned and moved his head a little but still didn't open his eyes. She soaked the cloth again and held it to a cut on his lip. His mouth opened and he began to suck the water from the cloth thirstily.

"That's it, my love," she said, feeling a surge of hope. She filled the bucket's ladle with water and held it to his lips, and he drank. His eyes opened suddenly after swallowing a few gulps. He looked at Charlotte with amazement and hope.

"Drink some more," she said, and had a sudden flashback to the day they met, the day he ordered her to do the same.

He drank and then reached his hand up to touch her arm. "Are you real, Charlie, or am I dreaming?"

"I'm real, darling, and we need to get you out of here. Can you walk?"

Charlotte could tell that Max's mind was processing the information available to him, including the desperate edge to her tone that indicated they were not yet out of danger.

Max's gaze found Jim at the door. He struggled to his feet. Jim didn't look at Max, instead keeping his eye fixed on the door of the house, the gun in his hand for immediate use. "Glad you finally woke up," he said, his voice deeper than how Charlotte remembered it.

"Are you two here alone?" Max asked, incredulous. "Didn't you bring the marshal?"

"No, Max," Charlotte answered. "Simon left a note saying that if we did he would..." She choked out the last words. "Kill you."

"Is that my gun?" Max asked as he walked unsteadily toward the front of the barn with his arm around Charlotte's shoulders. "Where's Simon?"

Jim didn't answer Max's first question about the gun. "He's inside the house. I'm going to shoot him when he comes out."

Max leaned against a beam near the door where Jim stood. "Give me the gun, Jim."

Jim turned his head to look at him then, his eyes shooting daggers. "Like hell I will, Max. This is my fight, not yours." He returned his gaze to the house.

"Jim," Charlotte said in a pleading voice. "Do as Max says."

Jim ignored her. Max stood upright from the beam and walked to where Jim stood. He placed one hand on his shoulder and reached down. He wrapped his hand slowly over the barrel of the gun, and Jim let it go without further resistance.

"You and Charlotte already saved my life, son. That's enough heroics for one day."

"We haven't saved it yet," Charlotte hissed. "Simon is still in the house."

"He's not much of a threat now that I'm untied and armed," Max responded, "but we might as well get out of here."

The three of them walked out of the barn and headed for the path.

"Go up ahead," Max said to them, placing himself between his two rescuers and the house. He walked backwards with his gun trained on the front door as they moved away. Simon didn't make an appearance. When the house was out of sight, Max stuffed his gun in his trousers, and they walked the quarter mile to the horse without incident.

Max untied the mustang from the tree and held the reins. He looked at Jim and Charlotte with confusion when they didn't make a move to mount. "Go on," he said. "What are you two waiting for?"

"Waiting for you to mount the damn horse," Jim growled. "If you honestly think I'm going to ride instead of you when your head is bashed and you're bleeding, you have another think coming."

Max stared at him. "All right, Jim. Geez." He mounted. "Land's sake, when did you get such a mouth on you, son?"

"You're pissing me off," Jim replied. "And I was scared as hell Simon had…" He didn't finish the sentence. Charlotte could hear the trace of a sob that choked back his words.

Max heard it too. "No worries, Jim. We're safe now, and Simon will pay for what he's done to all of us."

CHAPTER TWELVE

Max was right. The marshal arrested Simon later that day, and he informed them after they signed their statements that Simon would likely go to prison for a long time, now that he'd committed kidnapping and a violent crime that could be proven.

The doctor bandaged Max's head and attended to his other wounds, then instructed Charlotte to observe him overnight. She held his hand all night long and watched him sleep, waking him every once in a while to assure herself he was alive.

Max woke up the next morning in a foul temper. He demanded that Charlotte make his eggs a certain way and not screw them up like she did the last time, and he yelled at Jim for leaving the door open when he left to feed the horse. Jim and Charlotte exchanged looks and rolled their eyes behind his back every time Max barked an order or scolded them for a petty reason, but they did his bidding in silence without argument. They were both so happy he was alive they would have done anything he asked, and they suffered his ill temper in good humor, grateful just to hear his voice, loud and snarly though it was that morning. Charlotte suspected it was more than a headache that had put him in such a bad mood, and they finally learned what was truly bothering him when they sat down to lunch. He ignored the food on his plate and bellowed at them, pounding his fist on the table once before speaking.

"The next time I'm captured by a raving lunatic, I expect you two to bring the marshal, not come alone to rescue me. Got it?"

Jim leaned back in his chair, folded his arms in front of his chest, and glowered at Max.

"I believe I already told you about the note," Charlotte said tersely, matching Jim's defiant attitude. "Simon said he would kill you if we brought the marshal."

"Goddamn it, Charlie. You think he would've *not* killed me as a way to say thanks for being so obedient? If you wanted to pay mind to Simon's note and not bring the marshal, you could have at least brought a man. Blazes! A woman and a boy, rescuing me. Of all the nonsense. I would never have forgiven myself if..." Max rubbed his forehead, growing more agitated. "My god, the things he said he would do, I can't remember if they were part of my nightmares when I was passed out or if he really did say them."

Charlotte touched his arm. "Max, my love?" she said gently.

"What, darlin'?" he responded, his voice fraught with anxiety and frustration.

She waited a few moments before speaking, and the only noise they heard in that time was the ticking of the clock. When she answered, she spoke softly. "I did bring a man—a brave one. And Jim brought a capable woman. We're brave and capable partly because of you, because you've always believed in the both of us."

Max frowned at her, then shifted his gaze to Jim, who regarded him with narrowed eyes that dared him to disagree. Max groaned and ran his hand around the beard growing on his face. "You're right, Charlie," he said finally.

Jim's glower turned into a smile at Max's subtle admission. He stood. "Speaking of, I have brave, manly things to do. Like goin' on a picnic with the seamstress and her daughter that I was invited to when I delivered the hangers. I'll be off unless you have anything else to yell at me about, Max, in addition to saving your life."

Max got the sheepish look on his face that Charlotte secretly found adorable.

"I reckon anything else can wait until after your picnic," Max said gruffly. "And if you bring me one of Marta's sweet rolls, I'll forget the whole thing."

Jim grinned. He said goodbye and left the cabin. Charlotte and Max ate their lunch in silence. When they finished, Charlotte cleared the dishes off the table and washed them in the basin. She stopped scrubbing when she felt Max's arms wrap around her. He held her gently against his chest and kissed the side of her neck.

"So," he said in a deep voice close to her ear. "My wife thinks it's acceptable to put herself in danger on my behalf, does she?" He peppered her neck and ear with soft kisses.

"Yes," she squeaked.

He nipped her earlobe. "I disagree. You must be punished for that."

"Max, that's not fair. I don't think—"

"It doesn't matter what you think." His kisses became more demanding as they traveled over her shoulder. "I decide what's acceptable and what isn't," he said in between nips and kisses.

Charlotte whimpered with desire. He released her all at once, and she whimpered again when her body lost contact with his.

"Meet me in the bedroom for your punishment, young lady," he said before he left the room.

A wave of arousal washed over her body at the same time her mind protested the injustice of being punished for helping her husband. She slowly dried her hands. Taking a deep breath, she walked into the bedroom to find Max seated on the edge of the bed. He regarded her with his fierce eyes. "Over my lap, wife."

"But Max, you shouldn't exert yourself. You've been injured. Your wrists—"

"My wrists are fine enough to tan your hide."

Charlotte proceeded to provide him with her next excuse. "I didn't do anything wrong by coming for you. I don't deserve punishment."

"Are you going to make me come get you?"

Charlotte's temper flared at his refusal to reason. "Something happened to your head when it got hit, Max. You're addled."

"One."

She stomped her foot. "You're intolerable!"

"Two."

"Just how high are you going to count to?"

"Three."

"Very good, Max. You should teach math to my students."

He let out a growl and pounced. She squealed as he dragged her to the bed and dropped her on top of it. He straddled her. "Just for that, you're going to be fully naked when I redden your disobedient, impertinent bottom," he informed her with a mischievous glint in his eye. He proceeded to tear the dress off her body.

Charlotte watched his face with no small amount of awe as he stripped her with deft hands. When she lay naked on the bed, her clothes in a heap in a corner of the room, he captured a nipple in his mouth and flicked it with his tongue. He fondled her other breast, squeezing and pinching until she arched into his touch.

He removed his mouth from her breast to say, "My wife has a hard time obeying, doesn't she?"

He didn't wish to hear an answer because he kissed her when she tried to speak. The warmth of his mouth sent a current through her, and she reached up to wrap her arms around his neck. He grabbed each of her wrists and pinned them high above her head on the bed.

His lips unlocked from hers. "My wife must learn how I feel about a few things." Max lifted himself off of her and sat on the edge of the bed again. "And she must learn them over my lap. This instant."

Charlotte sighed and crawled to the position he wished her to take. She felt his cock pressing into her stomach and she squirmed a little over it, knowing it would drive him crazy.

"That's dangerous, my love," he rumbled.

His hand settled on her bottom and slowly stroked around the curve to the apex of her legs. He felt the slick proof of her desire. "Mm, naughty girl." He planted a swat on her left cheek. It wasn't a gentle swat, but it wasn't hard either.

"That's for disobeying me when I told you to come to me for punishment." He rubbed the place where he'd swatted before bringing his hand down on her other cheek. "And that's for calling me intolerable. I prefer 'darling'."

Charlotte moaned. The two swats had sent jolts of pleasure to the lowest part of her belly.

Spank. "That's for saving my life." His hand ran down one of her long legs and back up, then smacked her again. "That's for being brave in the face of danger on more than one occasion."

"Oh, Max," Charlotte sighed.

She understood finally. This was her husband's way of thanking her for rescuing him despite his displeasure over how it happened. Max spanked her mildly for many things, including how smart she was, how fetching she looked in her impractical dresses, and how cute she was when she stormed about sassing him. She laughed and cried over each ridiculous reason for being punished.

He landed one final hard swat and said sternly, "That's for being so darn loveable, Charlotte. It's hard on a man's heart, you know."

She choked out a laugh through her emotional tears. He lifted her, then pushed her to the middle of the bed, shucked off his clothes, and lay down with her. He pulled her into his arms and kissed her soundly. Charlotte wrapped her arms around his neck and met his passionate kiss with one of her own. When their lips unlocked, he moved his kisses south, starting from between her breasts down to her bellybutton.

"You didn't have to spank me," she said. "You could have just said thank you."

He moved his kisses to between her legs and

licked along her slit up to her engorged bundle of nerves. "That wouldn't have made you this wet, naughty girl."

He teased her clit with his tongue until her desire grew to massive heights. "Come for me, darlin'," he said. She shattered, arching her back and grasping the quilt with both hands as she did.

Breathing hard after her moans of release, she threaded her fingers through his hair. "I came for you," she said breathlessly.

"I know you did, darlin'." He moved his body over hers and looked deeply into her eyes. "Thanks for coming for me, my love."

Charlotte smiled, understanding the double meaning of his words. Her hips thrust forward as he invaded her core. He took her hard and fast, with both love and fury, grasping her hips to drive himself into her. Just as she was about to come again, he pulled out and flipped her around to take her pussy from behind. He landed hard swats on her sore cheeks as he ravished her, and she moaned at the pain and pleasure his body brought hers. She understood that this was both reward and punishment that he was inflicting, his feelings of love and consternation clear in every movement.

"You're mine," he growled in her ear. "And you will obey me and keep yourself safe from now on. Yeah?"

"Mm hmm," she moaned in the affirmative. He cracked his palm against her right cheek to drive the message home. She came again in that moment. He held fast to her shoulder and rode her hard until his desire built and he erupted. Groaning, he came deep inside of her.

After, Charlotte lay in Max's arms in a state of perfect happiness. She fell asleep thinking about the day that they met, the day he'd first come for her, and how lucky she was that he had.

EPILOGUE

Simon died in prison during the time that Jim attended college in New York. Following his graduation, Jim became a lawyer and one of the founders of the New York Society for the Prevention of Cruelty to Children, the first-ever agency devoted entirely to child protection. News of the NYSPCC spread, and soon some three hundred child protection associations were scattered across America. Jim left New York and founded one of the societies in Dallas in 1904.

While away at college, Jim kept in close contact with Max and Charlotte, and also with the seamstress's daughter, Clara. Jim and Clara married and settled in Dallas, a two-day journey by buggy from Max's and Charlotte's home in Porter, and much less than that when Jim bought Max and himself Ford automobiles in 1907.

Charlotte gave birth to five children over the years, three girls and two boys, the eldest of which joined Max in his trade, which by then had evolved from blacksmithing to all but entirely carpentry. His son possessed a unique talent for art and design, so they not only built quality furniture using Max's talents, but also breakthroughs in style using his son's. Their furniture became widely popular and replicated for years to come.

Charlotte's mother came to live with Max and Charlotte a couple of years after they married, and the arrangement couldn't have worked out better for everyone. Charlotte's mother escaped her unkind husband, and Charlotte's and Max's children gained a doting grandmother who minded them when Charlotte taught classes in Porter.

The love Max and Charlotte felt for each other only grew, as did the amount of time Charlotte spent over Max's lap. She never fully lost her stubborn pride, but it was kept in check, since neither did her husband lose the firmness in his right hand or the willingness to smack it across his wife's bottom when warranted.

All turned out well for Max, Charlotte, Jim, and the friends and family who surrounded them. They loved, laughed, and flourished, and they owed it all to one simple errand that Max accepted: the not entirely unpleasant task of fetching a lovely, vexing woman.

The End

BOOKS BY THIS AUTHOR

Caught By The Lawman

A scared young woman accused of theft stands in front of Marshal Jake Huntley's desk at the jailhouse. The lawman generally has no tolerance for criminals, but when she focuses her doleful blue eyes on him in a way that makes his heart race, he wants nothing more than to protect her.

Elizabeth Matthews is in desperate need of help, but she refuses to tell the truth when the marshal demands it. It's his job to protect people, but it's also his job to punish criminals, so how can she?

Though the lawman doesn't plan to use the law against her, he's not opposed to delivering justice in the form of a hard, bare-bottomed spanking over his knee. After her bottom is thrashed to a deep shade of crimson, her secrets spill out. Will the marshal be able to save her from enemies on both sides of the law?

Her Gruff Boss

The man Anna Brown comes to work for is not the amiable man she once knew. This version of Carter Barnes is gruff, impatient, and seems to be doing his best to ignore Anna's very existence.

And she's not putting up with it for one second longer.

An uncharacteristic display of temper from Anna seems to shock Carter out of his apathy, much to her delight. Even his discipline, which leaves her bottom red and burning, excites her in ways she's never known.

But a villain's vicious attack shatters Anna's newfound happiness, and the fallout sends her fleeing from the home. When Carter follows, she's forced to decide whether to trust him with her heart and return to the life they've built together...

Or turn her back for good on the only man she's ever loved.

Bringing Trouble Home

Widowed rancher Heath Wolfe worries he's making a big mistake by bringing Willow McAllister home to his ranch. A known troublemaker around town, she can't seem to keep a job or avoid skirmishes with the law, so the town marshal implores Heath to help. While Heath agrees to employ Willow, he certainly won't allow misbehavior, and he's even prepared to take the willful young lady over his knee for a sound spanking if warranted.

Orphaned and alone for several years, nineteen-year-old Willow is used to taking care of herself. She sleeps wherever she can find a soft surface and roams freely. She doesn't drink whiskey every night and she only steals when she has to, so it doesn't seem fair when the marshal insists she give up her freedom to work for Heath. She suspects that the rancher is as humorless as he is handsome.

Heath and Willow are as different as two people can be, but a tentative friendship forms. Old habits die hard, though, and it doesn't take long for Willow to engage in familiar shenanigans. When problems arise, will Heath regret bringing trouble home, or has Willow finally found a man who can steer her straight?

When He Returns

Proud and independent, thirteen-year-old orphan Wade Hunter doesn't want a family. But when the town marshal catches him stealing, Wade's given only two choices: Spend time in jail or become the marshal's ward.

Sadie Shaw, the marshal's eldest daughter, doesn't want another sibling. She has enough brothers and sisters, and she's dismayed when her kindhearted pa brings home another lost child. It doesn't help that this one is surly and arrogant. Worse, he thinks that because he's older, he's under no obligation to mind her household rules.

Wade and Sadie battle wills often as they grow into adulthood, burgeoning both their dislike for each other and their grudging respect. When faced with a problem that requires their unity, will they be able to set aside their differences, or will the strife they face only tear them apart for good?

Taming Tori

Proud and independent, thirteen-year-old orphan Wade Hunter doesn't want a family. But when the town marshal catches him stealing, Wade's given only two choices: Spend time in jail or become the marshal's ward.

Sadie Shaw, the marshal's eldest daughter, doesn't want another sibling. She has enough brothers and sisters, and she's dismayed when her kindhearted pa brings home another lost child. It doesn't help that this one is surly and arrogant.

Worse, he thinks that because he's older, he's under no obligation to mind her household rules.

Wade and Sadie battle wills often as they grow into adulthood, burgeoning both their dislike for each other and their grudging respect. When faced with a problem that requires their unity, will they be able to set aside their differences, or will the strife they face only tear them apart for good?

Mary Quite Contrary

Nineteen-year-old Mary Appleton manages a successful restaurant in the small town of Thorndale. Though passionate about cooking, she's naïve about the dangers of the world and innocent when it comes to love and romance.

Benjamin Gray, the stern new deputy in town, knows the restaurant is vulnerable to robbers, and his protective instincts ignite when he notices that Mary doesn't safeguard her money. When she refuses to lock up the cash in her register, Deputy Gray gives her only one other choice: Accept a hard spanking over his knee.

To Mary's surprise, the punishment does nothing to quell her attraction to Ben. Rather, she finds herself smitten by her older lover who brings her as much pleasure as pain. But will she accept his advice when it matters most, or will her contrary behavior ruin them both?

Handling Susannah

Rancher Adam Harrington wants to marry a wholesome, virginal bride with a sweet disposition. When he reads a young woman's unusual advertisement requesting a mail-order cowboy as her groom, he thinks they might be a good match, so he writes her a telegram. She pens a favorable response, accepting him as her future husband.

Susannah Smith's father bequeathed his ranch to her, but it was under one condition: She must be married. For Virginia City's fallen woman, finding a man to marry is no easy feat. The men in town who seek to court the hot-tempered, unwed mother are sluggards and drunks, not the kind of men capable of running a ranch. Desperate to find a suitable husband or else lose everything, she expands her search by listing an ad in the paper.

Adam and Susannah meet, and the attraction between them is undeniable, but it is soon followed by wariness. Susannah had planned to marry a man who would do her bidding, not take over everything. It's her ranch, after all. Equally befuddled, Adam thought he'd be marrying a woman who knows her place, not a temperamental brat who could benefit from some time over his knee.

Susannah feels outraged by Adam's authoritative ways, but his dominant handling in the bedroom leaves her trembling with desire. Will she learn to accept his firm leadership and expectations? And will Adam grow to love the woman who differs so drastically from the kind of wife he thought he wanted?

Catching Betsy

Betsy Blake yearns for love and romance, but the unattached men of Virginia City are crude, rough cowboys without the gentlemanly qualities she desires. She pens an advertisement in the paper for a mail-order groom from the east, specifying that he be well-dressed and mannerly.

Roderick Mason's reputation as an architect in New York City has earned him great success, but he hasn't been as lucky in love. The women of his circle are too prim and predictable for the adventurous rake. He longs for excitement and a woman who will challenge him. When he reads Betsy's ad in the paper requesting a gentleman groom, he's intrigued, so he heads west to meet her.

Roderick and Betsy are immediately smitten, but they soon discover that not everyone in Virginia

City is pleased by their match, especially one man who wants Betsy as his own. As Betsy's stalker becomes increasingly threatening, Roderick realizes he will go to great lengths to protect his sweet little country girl, including taking her over his knee for some painful discipline when she misbehaves or puts herself in danger. Will Betsy learn to face her problems and accept Roderick's love and discipline, or will he never succeed at what he desires most--protecting and catching Betsy?

Justice For Elsie

Hell-bent on revenge, orphaned rancher Elsie Fin rustles cattle from her neighbor, who she blames for her father's untimely death. She's so successful at stealing that she doesn't stop even when the local marshal gets suspicious. Instead, she decides what she needs is a loyal husband to protect her from the law, so she places a mail-order groom advertisement in the paper.

While seeking her groom, Elsie hires Wyatt Parker to help her around the ranch. Little does she know, he's actually an undercover deputy tasked with gaining her trust and verifying the marshal's suspicion of her theft.

Wyatt never imagined a beautiful, sweet woman like Elsie would be the mastermind behind such a serious illegal activity. To his way of thinking, she's more deserving of a spanking than life in prison. He wants to figure out how to save her, but will Elsie end up behind bars or married to her mail-order groom before he can?

Printed in Great Britain
by Amazon

31045849R00088